RADICAL RED

RADICAL RED

JAMES DUFFY

CHARLES SCRIBNER'S SONS • NEW YORK
Maxwell Macmillan Canada • Toronto
Maxwell Macmillan International
New York • Oxford • Singapore • Sydney

Charles Scribner's Sons Books for Young Readers
Macmillan Publishing Company
866 Third Avenue
New York, NY 10022

Maxwell Macmillan Canada, Inc.
1200 Eglinton Avenue East
Suite 200
Don Mills, Ontario M3C 3N1

Macmillan Publishing Company is part of the Maxwell Communication
Group of Companies.
First edition
Printed in the United States of America
10 9 8 7 6 5 4 3 2 1

Library of Congress Cataloging-in-Publication Data
Duffy, James, date.
    Radical Red / James Duffy. — 1st ed.
        p.   cm.
    Summary: The life of a twelve-year-old Irish girl living in Albany, New York, in the
1890s undergoes many changes when she and her mother become involved with Susan B.
Anthony and her suffragists.
    ISBN 0-684-19533-X
    1. Anthony, Susan B. (Susan Brownell), 1820–1906—Juvenile fiction. [1. Anthony,
Susan B. (Susan Brownell), 1820–1906—Fiction. 2. Women's rights—Fiction.
3. Irish Americans—Fiction. 4. Albany (N.Y.)—Fiction.] I. Title.
PZ7.D87814Rad   1993
[Fic]—dc20   93–12568

For Priscilla

RADICAL RED

CHAPTER ONE

"Stay in line," Sister Mary M. warned. "Stay in line and don't talk until you reach the sidewalk or it's back into the schoolhouse with the lot of you."

Sister Mary M. meant it, Connor knew. She was the toughest of the three Marys. Sister Mary C. and Sister Mary F. said the same as Sister Mary M., but they didn't always mean it. Sister Mary F. sometimes even shouted after them, "Go, girls, go!" when the line of brown uniforms reached the pavement. She would watch smiling as the girls scattered along the roadside like startled sparrows.

No talking for the boys, either. They straggled from the boys' door under the threatening glare of the principal, sullen and silent until the schoolyard lay behind. At the road they broke into wild shouting packs, laughing, pushing, and swearing under their breath about the school and the sisters. They raced above the banks of the Beaverkill,

I

the braver ones scrambling down the chalky slopes to see what the spring rains had washed up since the day before.

Connor envied them. They were free. Just once, she thought, to stumble and slide down the gray sticky bank and jump from rock to rock along the edge of the frothy stream. Just once to go home like the boys, her boots soaking and her wool socks and heavy jumper smeared with clay.

Last week, she remembered, her cousin Keefe had dared her to join the group of boys stumbling down the path. "Come on, Connor," he'd taunted. "You have a boy's name. See if you can do a boy's job."

Just once! Connor was tempted just once to stand in the churning water until it sloshed inside her boots. To grab a stick and poke it into the chalky suds. To throw a stone across the stream. *Just once* to push the nasty-tongued Keefe down the slope and laugh as he clawed at the clay to stop himself. And, most of all, to show herself wet and muddied to her father when he came home from work, to tell him that she was one of the boys. "Ah"—to hear him say— "my girl is become one of the boys. Look at her, Nora, she's been down to the Beaverkill with Keefe and the boys. She's as dirty as a pig."

Just once!

CHAPTER TWO

CONNOR AWOKE FROM HER REVERIE; THE BOYS AND GIRLS had fled. Across the road Doreen waved and shouted, "Tomorrow!" Connor tightened the strap around her books and slung them over her shoulder. Sister Mary Francis had lent her a tattered third-grade reader for Ma to work with. "See if your mother is up to this book yet," Sister Mary F. had said. "It's a good deed you're doing, Connor. A woman who can't read these days is only half a woman. And don't forget, mind you, to keep at her on her sums."

Ma knew her sums already but only in her head. She knew them as well as Mr. Flannery at the grocery store. And a whole lot better than her father who *had* been to school. "For all the good it did me." He laughed. "All I learned was which end of the newspaper was up." Ma's trouble was with the writing of the sums.

Connor turned down the hill toward the Hudson River.

The dirt walk and the road they called Madison Avenue followed the Beaverkill on its twisting way to the falls. Heavy carts labored up the road from downtown. An occasional shiny black carriage rolled along the road, the driver in his livery snapping a whip across the back of the sleek groomed horse. Sometimes the fragrance of perfume lingered in the afternoon air when a lady was on her way to tea at one of the fancy houses on Arbor Hill.

As she turned at Swan Street, Connor paused to gaze down the avenue to where they were making the new park. She wondered if the shack where she had been born and lived for ten years was still there. From this distance she wasn't certain which of the shanties in the Martinville slum had been the house of Donal and Nora and Connor O'Shea.

What Connor did remember was the man from the city in his heavy black suit, a gold chain across the buttons on his vest and a derby hat tilted to one side, who shouted at the families gathered in the muddy street, "You people have got to move. The city will be laying a park over your filth. You can take your geese and goats over to Canal Street. There's places for you there."

The shantytown was condemned, Connor remembered. That was the word the man from the city used, *condemned.* Other words, too, like *unsanitary* and *nasty* and a *menace to health.* Two years ago, almost to the day—on her tenth birthday—Donal and Nora and Connor had loaded their belongings into a rough cart behind an old gray horse and moved to Canal Street into four small rooms on the top floor of a tippy wooden tenement.

There was no place on Canal Street, ordinary as it was,

for Paddy the goat. "The goat stays here," Da had said. "He can live in the fancy park with the hoity-toity." He promised the tearful Connor that Paddy would be safe enough. "Goats can look after themselves, that's their way," Da assured her.

Connor shaded her eyes. There weren't any goats or geese poking among the wreckage of the shacks and tenements, only a handful of men tearing down the last of the buildings and filling wagons with boards and rubbish. Connor sighed and headed across Swan toward the capitol.

CHAPTER THREE

AT THE TOP OF STATE STREET THE SQUARE LITTLE CAPI-
tol building sat like an ugly toad. It was not much bigger
and not half so fine, Connor imagined, as some of the
mansions on Arbor Hill or around Washington Park.
Maybe today Da would take her down the hill to see how
the new capitol was coming along. "In a couple of years,
maybe by 1896 or '97, Connor, my girl, I'll be doing my
duty there," her father boasted, "in the new capitol of New
York State, the biggest and richest capitol building in all of
the country. You will be proud of your old da then."

Connor was already proud of him. Her father was the
sergeant of the capitol police. Someday he would be the
captain. "We have to see to it," Ma said. "Let's hope that
he's the man for the job." Every morning Ma took a warm
iron to Da's brass-buttoned jacket. She laid it across the
kitchen chair for Connor to brush while Da was lacing his
boots. Ma held the jacket for him to slip into over his wool

shirt. Then Connor began the buttons at the bottom and Da started at the top. They raced to the odd button, the thirteenth, in the middle of the jacket. Connor almost always won. Da bent down to tickle her cheek with his bristly mustache, did the same for Ma, and thumped down the steps to Canal Street.

Shading her eyes against the afternoon sun, Connor looked to see if Da was waiting for her on the capitol steps. Her father was not in sight. The assembly is in session, and he's needed inside, she thought. "They couldn't keep it going without me, Senator Phelan says," her father had told her. "Many's the time I've had to gather the assemblymen up from the saloons or the Delavan House, where a lot of them board during session, and drag them up the hill and put them at their desks so as Senator Phelan can tell them how to vote."

Connor knew Senator Phelan, a busy, bossy little man with red hair and a quick smile. Sometimes he was on the steps in the afternoon with Da catching a breath of "the fine Albany air," he always said. He had a grand house on Arbor Hill. For as long as she could remember, Connor and her mother had gone on Friday afternoons with a heavy laundry basket filled with fresh wash to the Phelan house and waited while the maid, usually Agnes, took it inside and returned with the basket of the rough wash, sheets and towels and the maids' uniforms. Ma at one side of the basket and Connor at the other would carry it down to Canal Street.

At the end of the month it was Mrs. Phelan who came to the door, a black purse in her hand, to give Ma the money. She always asked the same question, "And how much is it this month, Nora?" Ma would always say, "Four dollars, ma'am." She lowered her eyes as she took the paper money and slipped it in her pocket. Then Mrs. Phelan would look at Connor as though it were the first time she had ever seen her. "I'll send a sweet for the girl," she'd say to Ma, and after a while the maid would bustle to the back door with a piece of hard candy for Connor.

As Connor ran toward the capitol square, a young woman held out a pamphlet. Connor stopped. "For me?" she asked. The woman nodded. She had an armful of them.

Connor studied the pamphlet. It wasn't a proper magazine like the ones Da sometimes brought home for her from the assembly rooms where they had been discarded. On the front was a drawing of a woman with her hands chained together. The chains looked like the handcuffs Da carried on his belt. At the bottom of the picture were some big letters: "Women Want the Vote." Puzzled, Connor handed the pamphlet back to the young woman.

The woman shook her head. "It's for your mother. Will you take it home to her?"

Just the night before at the table, Connor remembered, Da told her mother that some crazy women had come to town. "They've come right up to the capitol," he announced, "to tell the men in the assembly what to do."

"Do what, Donal?" Ma asked.

"Give them the vote, Senator Phelan told me. Fat chance of that, eh, girl?"

Ma shook her head. "I don't understand these things." She gathered the plates for the dishpan.

"You don't have to worry your head about it," Da said.

"Senator Phelan will see to it for you. He'll have us send them packing. You can count on it."

Was this one of the crazy women? She looked nice enough. She had a red ribbon on her bonnet, some lace at the collar of her dress, and fine leather gloves.

"My mother doesn't read very well," Connor answered. "You'd better take it back, thank you."

"What is your name?" the woman asked.

"Connor, ma'am. Connor O'Shea."

"And how old are you, Connor?"

"Twelve years old, ma'am. I have to be on my way now."

The woman took her arm gently. "I'm Bertha, and I'll be twenty-five tomorrow. I'll bet you can read those books you are carrying."

"Yes," Connor admitted. "I'm trying to help Ma learn," she added proudly.

"Would you read this to your mother, please, Connor? It's important. For her, and for you too."

"I don't know, miss. I'd better not. Da—my father, I mean—he might not like it." Connor held out the pamphlet until the woman accepted it.

The woman smiled. "I'm sorry, Connor. Another time, perhaps. I'll be here for a while."

"Yes, ma'am." Connor smiled at Bertha and turned toward the capitol.

CHAPTER FOUR

DA WAS ON THE STEPS OF THE CAPITOL NOW. HE MUST have been watching while Connor talked to the young woman. He scowled at Connor. "Looking for a strapping, girl?"

Connor held her breath. She had almost forgotten about the strappings. She shivered at the memory. Saturday nights, sometimes other nights, when he came up from the tannery, Da used to stop at the public saloon with his friends. He drank too much. Connor remembered how he'd stumble into the shack at Martinville, face red and angry, to slump at the table and demand his supper. Silent, holding back her tears, Ma would serve him the warmed-over stew which, like as not, Da would taste and hurl to the floor. "Can't you cook, woman? You're not in the old country now. Look at the floor. Clean it up." Ma would just stand against the wall, staring hard at him, her arms folded against the punches she knew would come next. When

10

Connor screamed, Da would yank the belt from his britches and lay the strap across her bottom.

Afterward, her mother would come to Connor's cot in the corner of the bedroom to hold her until she fell asleep. Da would be snoring on the bed. "You mustn't mind, child," Ma would whisper. "It's only me your da is angered with. He will be all right in a while. He's not a bad man, your da."

Later Da got the job with the police at the capitol and didn't drink so much, and the punching and the strappings stopped. "He's come to accept it," her mother told Connor. "It's more children he wants, like his cousin Kevin, and I can't give them to him. You have to be his boy, Connor. He had the name waiting for you, thinking you were certain to be a boy. 'We'll still call her Connor,' he said when you were born."

"What's the matter?" Connor asked her father timidly. "I only stopped to talk." She was afraid now. Da had taken to drinking again with a few of his men after work. He'd come home some nights red in the face, stare silently at Ma and her, and stumble into the bedroom. Ma would take his plate to the icebox.

"She gave you one of her filthy papers. I saw you," Da accused her.

"I didn't take it, Da. I gave it back."

"See that you don't touch one again, or it will be the strap, twelve years old or no."

Senator Phelan had come out to breathe the Albany air. He smiled at Connor. "Trouble with the family, Donal?" he asked pleasantly.

"Yes, sir. I mean, no, sir. I was telling my girl to stay

away from the crazy women. They come here to cause us trouble, you said."

"Well, perhaps I was a bit harsh. I don't suppose they'll do any harm. We have to put up with our women sometimes, don't we, Donal?"

"That we do, Senator. You spoke the truth there. Why don't we keep them off the streets? A couple of the boys and I could send them packing in no time. Just give me the word."

"The streets are public, Donal. They belong to everyone who's not causing a disturbance. That's the law. We have to put up with them on the sidewalk. But not into the capitol, mind you. That's what they have in mind, I have no doubt, marching into the assembly rooms. We can't have them there, Donal. You'll see to that, won't you?"

"Yes, sir."

"Why don't you and your girl go on down the street to see how the new building is progressing? It's quiet inside here." Senator Phelan strolled back into the capitol.

"There's a man for all the seasons, Connor. Inside they're talking that he could be governor someday. He was telling me this morning again they will be wanting a captain of police for the new capitol and he might be having a word with the authorities. Captain O'Shea, girl! How does that sound?"

Along State Street they passed women holding pamphlets out to the people passing by. Da straightened his shoulders and pushed out his chest. Once or twice it seemed to Connor he wanted to speak, to order the women to be on their way. The words, not spoken, turned into a growl.

12

"What's the vote, Da?" Connor asked.

"That's not your business," her father said sharply. He paused. "Well, if you want to know, it's going to the voting place and marking a piece of paper for the men we want to come to the assembly. The authorities count the votes and those men who get the most are selected. We can vote for the governor of the state and the president of the country, too. And for other things that come up, the senator says, like money things and the like."

"Do you vote, Da?"

Her father shook his head. He was embarrassed. "You have to be able to read a paper they call the Constitution or something, you see. If you can't do that, you don't get the vote."

"I could read it for you," Connor said. "Sister Mary Francis says I can read better than any of the boys. Can I vote?"

"You have to be twenty-one too. If you dress up like your cousin Keefe, they might give you the piece of paper." Her father laughed. "You have a boy's name, right enough, and if you cut your hair, you'd look like a boy."

"What about Ma? She can read the second-grade reader, most of it."

"Your ma can't vote. No woman can vote, not even Mrs. Phelan if she wanted to, and she has been to a college for women."

"Why not?"

"Women don't know about the world. They don't have the experience, the senator says. You have to know what you are voting about and all those things. If I studied the words some more, I could read what they tell me to. But I don't need to learn. Senator Phelan looks after the matter for me."

"But . . . " Connor began.

"Enough of the voting talk. Look up there at the second floor, at the corner of the building there. That will be where they are making the senator's office. And over there at the other corner is the governor's office. They can look all the way down to the Hudson to see the ships. How about that, girl?"

CHAPTER FIVE

MA WAS PULLING THE WASH OFF THE LINE STRUNG across the little porch at the back of the kitchen. "This time of year they won't dry inside and they won't dry outside, especially the uniforms. We were better off in Martinville where the sun could find the wash."

"So could Paddy," Connor said. She remembered that once in a while the goat took it into his head to drag Ma's sheets down into the mud. "I looked for him today—the geese too—but I think they were chased away. Did they eat the geese?"

Ma wasn't listening. "I'll have to iron these uniforms dry!" she muttered. "Bring up an armful of wood," she told Connor. "I'll need the fire for the irons."

Connor dropped her books on the drying room floor. When they moved to Canal Street, the little windowless box was to be Connor's room. It still was, she supposed, but pretty soon it got to be the drying room, and that was what it was called now. In the winter and when it rained and when the sun didn't shine on the back of the building, which was most of the time, Ma had to dry the wash on lines hung from wall to wall of Connor's room. "I can't help it, girl," Ma had said. "It's the only room we have." Sometimes on a Saturday and Sunday when Ma hadn't taken in extra wash, Connor had her room to herself, but it wasn't often.

"The parlor . . . " Connor had begun. They never used the little room at the front that Ma called the parlor. The door was always shut tight. Inside, it smelled like dust and stale furniture. After they had moved to Canal Street, Mrs. Phelan gave Ma an old sofa with two heavy chairs and a little black piano. Ma put them in the room she announced would be the parlor. She took twelve dollars from the wash money jar and went downtown to Swithenbanks furniture store and bought a flowered blue carpet for the floor. Later she paid four dollars for fancy lace curtains she put up on the narrow window looking down on Canal Street. And a dollar for some silk flowers she put in the vase on the piano.

Ma had shaken her head before Connor could finish the sentence. "We have to have someplace in our lives, girl, that's not the smell of the wash and dirty boots and cabbage." Even Da who spent all his time at home in the kitchen when he wasn't sleeping agreed. "It's the only fancy we have," he'd said. "We can't be living like the pigs and the goats."

At Christmastime Da's cousin Kevin and his wife, Peggy, came to sit in the parlor to take tea and currant cake. But not Connor or Keefe and his four rowdy brothers. The

16

boys banged around in the kitchen and leaned over the porch railing and kicked each other and shouted and rolled on the floor in their Sunday clothes until Peggy came in and gave them each a good knock on the head. "Savages" she'd called them. "Every one of you is headed straight for the jailhouse, and it won't be your da and I who will be coming down to get you out." She'd gone back into the parlor and closed the door. Keefe had stuck out his tongue and made an ugly sound.

Connor carried the wood basket to the first floor and through the hall to the back door. The people in the building kept their wood and coal in bins under the porch. Connor filled the basket and took it up to her mother. Wood was faster than coal in getting Ma's irons hot.

"Mrs. Phelan sent Kate—she's the one who does their fancy laundry at the house—to say they wanted the wash tomorrow instead of Friday. Your da will have to have his dinner cold if he comes home. You might make a plate for him, Connor. There's a bit of roast and potatoes and pudding in the box."

The brown icebox sat against the wall on the porch. In the summer the ice man brought a block of ice up the steps twice a week for the top of the box. The rest of the year it was cool enough on the porch to do without.

Connor watched her mother fold the old sheet she ironed on across the kitchen table. Ma licked her finger and touched the bottom of a heavy black iron she lifted from the top of the stove. The iron sizzled. The hot iron brought the smell of starch from the uniforms. Connor studied her sums, lifting her head from time to time as Ma put the cold iron on the stove, unsnapped the handle, and snapped it on a hot iron. The pile of folded uniforms in the clothes basket grew higher. She wondered how her mother could work so fast, hour after hour, bending halfway over the table.

"Can you read to me, child?" Ma asked. "We won't have time for our lesson tonight."

Connor brought in the third-grade reader Sister Mary F. had given her. "It's a different reader that Sister gave me. She says you ought to be ready for it by now. And she says you must start doing your sums. It doesn't matter if you know them in your head. You have to know how to write them, too, she says. You might want an office job someday. It's better, Sister says, than doing somebody's dirty wash."

Connor opened the book. It wasn't like the book she had used in the third grade. It looked more interesting. One section was legends, another was folktales, and the last was called historical stories. She studied the titles. "Here's one called 'The Emerald Princess.' It's Irish. I'll read it to you now, so tomorrow night you'll know the story when you read it to me."

The light in the kitchen grew dim. Connor's mother put the iron down and struck a match to the coal-oil lamp. She turned the wick high and put it on the table's edge next to Connor. From time to time she straightened up and rubbed her back while she listened for her husband's boots on the stairs. She shook her head and took up the iron. Darkness filtered into the kitchen.

Connor looked up, then continued reading about Deirdre, the Emerald Princess. The prince was sure to carry her off at the end. That's what always happened. The prince would come to steal her from her father or her wicked husband and sweep her up onto his horse, and they would gallop across the moor. Quickly Connor glanced through the pages ahead. It looked as though this story were different. Ma might not like that. Whenever Connor finished reading a story with a happy ending, Ma sniffled with pleasure. "That's not the way it is, girl, in real life, I can tell you that."

Downstairs someone slammed the heavy front door, which always made the house shake. Thick steps plodded up the stairs. Ma finished a pillowcase and pushed the irons to the back of the stove. She glanced at Connor who folded her hands in her lap. Ma moved to stand beside the table.

Da staggered into the room. He smelled of beer. He pulled his chair out from under the table and sat down heavily. His face was bloated and his eyes red. He had undone the top two brass buttons of his uniform. He stared up at Ma. "Where's my supper, woman?"

Connor's mother breathed deeply before answering. "You've been at the drink again, Donal O'Shea. You smell of beer and whiskey."

"It's my supper I want, not your scolding tongue, Nora Fitzmaurice. I've been drinking, that I have. Do you know *who* I've been drinking with, woman?"

"Conlan and his friends."

"Not tonight, my darling Nora, not tonight," Da said proudly. "Not in a public house, either, but at the Delavan House with Senator Phelan and his important friends who have come up from New York City. That's who I was with."

Ma turned aside. "I hope they're more sober than you, Donal. Get your da his plate, Connor."

Da lifted his leg for Connor to pull off his heavy boot. "We were making plans, we were," he mumbled. "We were making plans for the crazy women."

CHAPTER SIX

"IT'S RAINING OUT AGAIN THIS MORNING," CONNOR'S mother told her. "Put your father's old cape over you."

"It's too big, Ma, and the boys make fun of it, like they do of my boots. Everybody knows it's Da's old police cape. They'll start calling me a boy again, mostly Keefe and his friends. Why can't I have the umbrella?"

"Because I have to go over to the Delavan House to get some shirts. One of Senator Phelan's fancy friends doesn't like the way they do them at the hotel, so your da offered him my services. He says it will help him get to be the captain in the new capitol building."

Connor was silent. Da was always bringing shirts home from the capitol or sending Ma to the Delavan House or somewhere to fetch them. It made Ma mad. She had enough to do, she sometimes told Da, with the Phelans and her regular people. Afterward, she said to Connor, "It's not my way to complain, child, you know that. I married your da for better or worse. Someday, I hope, it will be for the better."

It was no time now to fuss about the old rubber shoulder cape. Let the stupid boys say what they liked. Most of them wore their das' old clothes, or their brothers'.

"Come straight home from school," Ma said. "We have to deliver Mrs. Phelan's wash."

The rain was only a drizzle. When she came to Madison Avenue, Connor slipped off the heavy cape and folded it over her arm. Sometimes, she knew, when one of the boys had to wear something he was ashamed of, he threw it down the bank into the Beaverkill. Do I dare? Connor asked herself. She could tell Ma it slipped off into the stream or that she'd put it down somewhere and it wasn't there later. But Ma wouldn't believe her. She wouldn't say so, but she would be disappointed. She'd look at Connor with sadness in her eyes. "Well," she might say, "we'll be having to get you another." The next day she might go over to the Delavan House to see if they had some wash so she would have the money to buy Connor a proper rain cape without taking the money from the wash jar. I can't do that to Ma, Connor told herself.

She wondered what the crazy women did when it rained. What did Da mean when he said the senator and his friends were planning to take care of them? Before Connor had drifted off to sleep beneath the lines of sheets, she had heard Ma say something to her father. Ma hadn't sounded like she was angry, more like she was asking him questions. Maybe it had to do with being captain of the police. Maybe they were talking about how they could move to a

22

proper house up the hill and Ma wouldn't have to do the wash anymore.

Doreen dashed across the road, thrusting her way among the carts and carriages rolling downtown. Doreen's father was a butcher with his own shop in the market section, and Doreen had both a black silk umbrella and a plaid rain cape. "Did you go to the capitol yesterday?" she asked straightaway. "What's going on there?"

Doreen and her father took a close interest in what went on in the capitol building. When Da let slip that such and such a drunken assemblyman had to be taken to his room in the hotel or there was a fistfight on the senate floor, Connor made sure to tell Doreen, who told her father. It wasn't often, Doreen's father said, that you could read about things like that in the newspapers. He relied on Connor to keep him informed about "all those shenanigans."

"Nothing much. Da showed me where the governor will have his office in the new building. It's still a good while before they move in. And he was at the Delavan House last night with Senator Phelan talking about the crazy women who have come to town. He said something else to Ma, but I didn't hear it." Connor didn't tell Doreen that Da came home drunk. "And," she said proudly, "I talked to one of the women. Bertha was her name. She was real nice. But I'm not supposed to, Da says. They are just here to make trouble."

"What are you talking about?" Doreen demanded. "I haven't heard about any crazy women."

"They want the vote, Da says."

"What vote?"

"The vote for women. They want to be able to vote in the state of New York for assemblymen and other things," Connor said with authority. It wasn't often she knew something, except for state-house gossip, that Doreen didn't know. Doreen always had her hand up in school before Connor could raise hers.

"Why don't they just go ahead and vote?"

"They can't. They aren't allowed to. It's because they're women and the law says they can't vote, only men, because they don't understand the things you have to vote for."

"I know as much as the stupid boys at St. Stephen's," Doreen said. "Maybe more. They can vote and I can't, is that what you're saying, Connor?"

"They can when they get to be twenty-one and you can't unless they change the law. The boys can't, either, if they can't write their names and read the Constitution, or part of it." I'd better not tell Doreen my father can't read it, Connor thought.

"Well, we can read it. We did in class last year, remember? We can ask the sisters about it."

"Maybe," Connor half agreed. "It's Sister Mary Francis who will talk to us. The others will only talk to you about your vocation. It sounds to me like you can be a nun or a nurse or a teacher when you grow up—or get married. That's about it."

"Let's ask Mary Francis, then. She thinks girls are better than boys, you can tell."

CHAPTER SEVEN

WHEN SCHOOL WAS OUT, CONNOR AND DOREEN WAITED for Sister Mary Francis to finish clearing off her desk. "What's the matter with you two?" the sister asked. "The others are halfway down the street by now."

Connor looked to Doreen. "You ask," she said.

"Well, we want to know about the vote. Connor says her father told her that women can't vote. We wanted to know for sure."

"Connor's right. They can't."

"I told you she would know," Doreen said to Connor. "Teachers know everything."

"I certainly don't know everything, but I can read and write and that's the start of what you need, especially if you are a woman. Some men read and write to vote, but not for much else. Some of the boys at St. Stephen's don't seem to care at all about learning. Especially your cousin Keefe, Connor."

25

It wasn't the first time the sister had spoken to her about Keefe. There wasn't anything Connor could do about him. His da and ma didn't care what happened to him. "There was this woman," she said to Sister Mary Francis, "at Swan and State who talked to me. Bertha was her name. She was giving out little pamphlets with the picture of a woman on the front. She was handcuffed."

"She must have been one of Susan B. Anthony's group," Sister Mary Francis said. "It was in the newspaper. They have come to town for the convention."

Connor was puzzled. "I don't understand." Da hadn't said anything about a convention, whatever that meant, or a woman called Susan B. Anthony. "What's a convention?" she asked.

Sister Mary Francis smiled. "It's kind of complicated. Sit down and I'll try to explain. Do you have to go home, Connor, to help your mother?"

"Pretty soon I do."

"I'll go as fast as I can. Women can't vote in the state of New York, where we live, or in most, though not all, of the other states, and they can't vote for the president of the United States anywhere. What do you think that means?"

"All the people elected are men," Doreen said.

"Right. This country is supposed to be a democracy. You both know about that, because I taught you last year. But women don't have any say in this democracy. So some women like Susan Anthony are trying to get the states to change their constitutions. And the U.S. constitution, too, you know what that is."

"The law." Doreen spoke again.

"In a way, yes. Anyway, every state has its own laws or constitution. To change them you have to call a convention. Delegates from New York State come to a special meeting here in Albany to decide about making a change. Assemblymen and others are the delegates, understand?"

Connor nodded. Now she could explain it to Ma. Senator Phelan would tell Da. "Are there women delegates?" she asked Sister Mary Francis.

"In other states there sometimes are, but I read in the paper they aren't allowing women to be delegates to the Albany convention."

"That's not fair," said Doreen. "Why not?"

"I'm not sure. I guess it's because the men don't want women to get the vote in New York. But you'll have to ask the women you see on the street corners, like Connor's friend Bertha. Or Connor can ask Senator Phelan when she sees him. You talk to him, don't you, Connor?"

"Yes. He's my father's friend. They were talking together last night at the Delavan House."

"So that's why the women are in town, to persuade people to support them at the convention. Susan B. Anthony—she's from Rochester—is in charge of the women. She'll be arriving soon from Kansas. They are having a convention there too. The women will probably have a parade in town. That's all I can tell you. I don't think the men want to give in."

"Are you going to parade, Sister?" Doreen asked.

Sister Mary Francis shook her head. "I'd like to, I really would, but I can't. Don't ask me why. That's another matter. Scoot on home now, the both of you. If someone gives you a pamphlet, bring it to school. I'd like to see it."

"I've got to run," Connor told Doreen. "Mrs. Phelan wants the wash a day early. See you tomorrow."

"Don't forget the pamphlet if you see the woman again. I want one, too."

"I'm not going that way," Connor called, and raced down Madison.

Ma had brought the basket down the stairs and was waiting impatiently at the front door. "I put the pillow slips in the small basket," she told Connor. "Run up and fetch it. My legs are going to give out on me climbing up and down those stairs for the water and the wood and the coal and wash. Where's your rain cape, lass?"

"At school. I stayed after to talk to Sister. I ran off and left it." Connor felt good that she could tell Ma the truth about the cape. She dashed up the steps two at a time, threw her books on the table, and ran down with the basket. She grabbed one end of the big basket, and together Ma and she headed for Arbor Hill.

"I'll bet I know what Da was doing last night at the Delavan House," Connor said.

"So do I. Drinking beer and whiskey with the senator. Your father has said more than once he wasn't going to touch the stuff, but. . . . That talk about crazy women coming to town, what kind of foolishness was that?"

"It's true, Ma," Connor said. She put down her baskets so she could shift hands.

"Here, give me the small basket. What's true is that Da was drunk, Senator Phelan or no Senator Phelan."

"They must have been making plans, just like he said. There's a big meeting—it's called a convention—at the state house, Sister Mary Francis told Doreen and me.

They're going to talk about the vote. Maybe there's going to be trouble. Sister didn't say so, but there could be."

"What vote is that, Connor?"

"The vote for women, Sister. That's what the women on the street are doing, trying to get the men to give them the vote too. Sister said I should tell you it's important. Women ought to have the vote, just like men."

"That's the man's business, girl. Anyway, your da doesn't have the vote. There's no reason for me to have it. What would I do with it? It's not going to feed us."

"It's your right, Ma. Da doesn't have the vote because he can't read the Constitution—that's the law of the country. He doesn't care because Senator Phelan tells him what to do. But you can read now, Ma, better than Da can. And you can write a little."

Connor's mother quickened her step. "We can talk about it later. First we have to get the wash up the hill. Lift your boots, child."

CHAPTER EIGHT

CONNOR CHEWED ON THE LAST BITE OF SODA BREAD AND washed it down with half a cup of tea and milk. Would Bertha be out with her pamphlets this early in the morning? Ma was already out on the rickety porch wringing a wet sheet over the edge. "Is it raining, Ma?" Connor called.

"The sun is trying to come up," Ma answered. "I'll hang the wash out today. There's no room on the lines inside."

"I'll go with Da, then," Connor said. On good days she sometimes walked to school by way of the capitol. It was longer than cutting across to Madison, but a lot nicer. They passed the houses of the rich, and she and Da talked about which ones they would live in when their ship came in.

She stood up to button Da's jacket. She strapped her books together and followed him down the steps. His heavy boots made the stairway tremble. Someday, Connor thought, the building will collapse into a pile of rubble, like the old shacks in Martinville. It was already tilting ten degrees, Da said, just like the tower they had over in Italy.

"Hurry up, girl. Senator Phelan will be coming in early. We have important matters to take up."

"About the crazy women?" Connor asked.

"I can't be talking about them with your ma and you. It's private business, secret government business, you might say."

It *was* about the women who were coming to Albany and the woman who was in charge, Connor bet. What was her name? Susan, Susan something or other. I'll ask Bertha if I have a chance, she thought.

From the capitol steps Connor could see Bertha in her bonnet, unless it was someone else, down at the corner of Swan and State. Da hurried up the steps. "You'd better run, girl," he warned. "The school bell will be ringing before you get there."

Connor ran toward Swan Street. For a second she paused to look back at the capitol. Da had disappeared inside. She was safe.

Bertha smiled. "On your way to school, are you, Connor?"

She's remembered my name, Connor thought happily. She knows who I am. "Could I have one of your pamphlets, please?" she asked. "I told my teacher and she wants to see one."

"I have a lot." Bertha laughed. "They are hard to get rid of. Not many people ask for one. They might take one to be polite, but they drop it on the pavement when they get down the street."

"I'll take one for my mother, too, then," Connor said. "And another for my friend Doreen."

"Goodness," Bertha said, "this is a big order. Are you sure you don't want one for yourself?"

The memory of Da's threat to take the strap to her flashed through Connor's mind. "Ma and I will read hers together," she said. "My teacher—Sister Mary Francis—says you are in the newspaper. You came to fight for the vote, she says."

"Maybe not to fight. Persuade, you can say, persuade the men to hear us at the convention so we can explain why women should be given—no, not given—I mean should *have* the right to vote. It's not charity, Miss Anthony said, it's our right. Anyway, I didn't have to come here. I already live in Albany."

Miss Anthony, that was it, Susan B. Anthony. Connor had it straight now; she could tell Ma. "And Sister said Miss Anthony is coming to town."

"Tomorrow night, that's right. On the train from Chicago. All the way from Kansas. There's a convention out there too. Will you be at the railway station, Connor? Bring your ma. We'll all be out there to welcome Aunt Susan. I'll introduce you and tell her you took these pamphlets."

"I'll see," Connor said. She imagined what Da would say if she and Ma went to the station. "Thank you for the pamphlets. I'm late now. I'll tell Sister and Doreen about Miss Anthony. They'll want to know."

Doreen was waiting anxiously. "Run," she shouted when she saw Connor. "The bell's about to ring."

"Here," Connor said, shoving a pamphlet at Doreen. "I have one for Sister Mary F. and one for my mother. The woman who's in charge, Susan B. Anthony she's called, is coming to Albany tomorrow night. On the train from Chicago!"

The bell sounded as they ran toward the door. Sister Mary Francis held it open for them. "Get to your seats," she whispered. "We'll talk after school."

Doreen stood on one side of the sister and Connor on the other as she turned the pages of the pamphlet. She pointed to a fuzzy picture of a woman with her hair pulled tight into a bun. "This is Aunt Susan," Sister told them. "That's what her girls, the young women who work with her, call Miss Anthony. Sometimes I feel like I'd like to be outside on the pavement with them."

"You can't, you said," Connor reminded her. "Because you're a nun, is that right?"

"Mostly. You and Doreen will have to take my place," Sister Mary Francis teased.

Again Connor remembered the strapping. "We're not old enough, are we?" she asked. She hoped the sister would tell her no.

"I don't know, Connor." Sister Mary Francis sighed. "Miss Anthony will need all the help she can find. The men at the capitol aren't going to give in. The newspaper says Senator Phelan is moving heaven and earth against suffrage."

"Suffrage?" Doreen asked.

"The right to vote, Doreen. Aunt Susan is in charge of the National-American Woman Suffrage Association. See, it's right here on the first page of the pamphlet. It's a long title, but it only means that women want the right to vote, same as men."

CHAPTER NINE

"MA?" CONNOR CALLED WHEN SHE CAME INTO THE kitchen. There was no response. Puzzled, Connor went out to the porch. Half-dry sheets were flapping in the cool spring breeze.

Where was her mother? She had never been gone before when Connor returned from school. As she dropped her books on the table, Connor noticed a torn piece of store paper. "Gon To Delivan Hows," Ma had printed in uneven letters with a crayon. Ma's starting to write, Connor thought happily. Now they could work on that together. Tomorrow she would tell Sister Mary F. And the sums, she mustn't forget those. If the crazy women got the vote, Ma could go to the capitol or wherever you put your vote and vote for Senator Phelan and Da's other friends. Maybe she wouldn't even vote for the senator if he kept on getting Da drunk or if he didn't make him captain of police.

Did you have to be good at your reading and writing and your sums, Connor wondered, to be a captain? She could teach Da too, if he'd let her. But he probably wouldn't. He never asked about her schoolwork, and once when she tried to read him something about Senator Phelan in one of the newspapers he'd brought home for starting the fire, Da was embarrassed and pushed the paper aside. "I know all about that, lass. From the senator himself," he grumbled. "Don't be uppity with me with your school ways. There's a lot of things in life you don't learn in a schoolroom."

Connor heard her mother hurrying up the steps. "You got here first, did you, child? I had to take the shirts back to your da's fancy friend."

"How much did he pay you?" Da brought home shirts for Ma to do for ten cents, though sometimes she was paid as much as twenty-five cents a shirt and once a senator from New York City gave Ma a whole dollar extra.

"Nothing. He wasn't in his room and he didn't leave payment with the hotel. I guess you can say I was helping Da get along with being a captain. Did you see my note?" Ma asked shyly.

Connor nodded. "It was on the table and I didn't see it at first because I put my books on it." She paused. She wasn't going to say there were mistakes in the writing. Later on they could make the corrections. Right now it was a note for the two of them. It must have been hard for her mother to bring herself to write it. Ma didn't mind reading out loud and adding sums in her head, but she was afraid to have Connor *see* her mistakes. But now she had begun, and that was what was important, Sister said.

Connor changed the subject. "I could have taken the shirts to the hotel for you," she said.

"I wanted to see the crazy women on the streets for

myself. Your da made them sound like wild beasts in the forest. Well, they don't look like crazy women any more than Mrs. Phelan does. Nice respectable women they are. Not like those painted women you see in the hotel. One of them gave me this." Connor's mother took a folded pamphlet from her apron pocket.

"I have one, too," Connor said. She showed her mother Bertha's pamphlet. "Look, they're just the same. Now we can read them together. Sister Mary Francis explained parts of it to Doreen and me."

"I'll make us a cup of tea," Connor's mother said. She lifted a lid from the top of the stove and poked the coals into a flame. "Let's see how the sheets and tablecloths are." She reached out the kitchen door. "Still damp. I'll have to take them down before the night comes on."

Connor opened her pamphlet to the picture of Aunt Susan. "This is Susan B. Anthony. They call her Aunt Susan. She's leading the women," she explained to her mother.

"She looks like an old woman," Ma said. "But you can't tell from the picture, can you?"

"She's over seventy, Sister told us. Tomorrow she's coming to Albany with more of her girls. That's what they call them, Aunt Susan's girls. I think Sister Mary Francis wishes she were one of them."

Connor's mother frowned. "She's a nun, child. That's a shameless thing for a sister to be saying."

"She's not like the other nuns, Ma. She's been to college, a real college, she says, not a teacher's college or a nun's school."

"There's no call for a sister talking like that."

36

"Like what, Ma?"

"Like wanting to be out on the street corners handing out pamphlets and talking to everyone who comes by."

"You said they looked nice, Ma, not like the painted women. You said they weren't crazy."

"They weren't nuns, Connor. That's what I'm talking about. Now let's see what the words say." She put her finger under the first words in the pamphlet. "'For more than a' . . . What's that word, child?"

Connor opened her pamphlet. "'For more than a hundred years,'" she read. "A hundred years. Spell it out, Ma."

"H-u-n-d-r-e-d. Hoon-dred."

"*Hun*dred, Ma, not *hoon*dred."

"All right, *hun*dred. 'For more than a *hun*dred years, wo-women have been p-prison . . . prisoners.'"

"Good, Ma. You said it right, 'prisoners.' See, right there on the front. The woman is in handcuffs, like the ones on Da's belt. 'Prisoners,' it says, 'in their own country.' Go on, Ma. I'm sorry I read it first."

"What does that mean, Connor? I'm not a prisoner."

Connor didn't know how to respond. She read the next sentence, and the next. That was what Sister Mary F. said to do. "If you don't understand, class, keep on reading and you might find out." The next sentence and the one after it began to explain. "Read it, Ma. It's going to tell you."

Slowly, with growing confidence, her mother read on. "'Prisoners, be-because they cannot vote.' Is that right, Connor?"

"It's right, Ma. Go on."

"'With-out the vote, women cannot' . . . What's that word, lass, 'con—'?"

"'Control.' Say it, Ma."

"'Cannot control their des-ti-ny.' What does that mean?"

"It means, I think it means . . . " Connor stammered. "It means your life. What you do in your life, like being free, I guess, and not a prisoner."

CHAPTER TEN

ON SATURDAYS MA CLEANED THE APARTMENT AND BAKED
the bread for the week ahead before she did the wash.
When Connor came into the kitchen rubbing the sleep
from her eyes, the bread was already on its first rising under
a dish towel on the back of the stove. By Thursday the
bread had usually been eaten, and her mother would then
make two loaves of soda bread, sometimes with currants, to
carry them through.

In an hour she'd have to bring up a scuttle of coal to mix
in with the wood. Sometimes in the spring Ma let the fire
die out in the evening. Coal was too dear to use when the
days were turning warm.

"I'll be making a raisin loaf for Sunday," Ma told
Connor. "Kevin told your da they might be coming by for a
cup of tea." Seeing Connor frown, she added, "Don't you be
worrying. Peg is leaving the boys home with Keefe. You can
sit in the parlor with the grown-ups if you take a liking."

39

Whenever Peggy came to visit, Connor noticed, Ma let herself talk as she had in the old country. The rest of the time she tried to speak like Da. "In America," he told Ma, "you have to speak American. You let them know you're Irish, and it won't take them long to look down on you. They will think you're the dirt of the earth. That's what Senator Phelan said."

"He's Irish, Donal. You said so yourself. So is Mrs. Phelan."

"That may be so, but it was his grandfather's father who came to Albany almost a hundred years ago. The senator is a Yankee by now, even if his da did grow up in Martinville. Now look at him, Senator Thomas Phelan, the leader of the New York State Senate with a big house on Arbor Hill and maybe someday to be the governor of the whole state. And he'll take me along, he says."

You could hardly tell from listening to Ma, Connor thought, that she had come over from the old country only fifteen years ago. It was her friend Peggy, who had left County Clare when she was Connor's age, who wrote to Nora about a Donal O'Shea who was looking for a real Irish wife like his cousin Kevin's. "They sent me the money for the passage," her mother had told Connor. "And I came and I talked to Donal and we were married. As simple as that it was."

"Did you love him, Ma?" Connor once asked. It seemed to her that Ma sometimes got a faraway look when she put the iron down to take a cup of tea with Connor in the late afternoon and talk about County Clare.

"When your da doesn't drink, he's the finest man in the

city. Even with drink inside him, he is still the handsomest."

That didn't answer her question, so Connor asked again, "Did you love Da, Ma?"

"I did, lass. But it didn't happen the way it does in your reading books, you understand. We weren't young lovers, and he wasn't from my village or even from my county. His people came over from Galway quite awhile ago. It was like I was a stranger to Donal and he to me when we decided to make a life together and have a family and a fine house like Peg and Kevin talked about. It was sort of a business arrangement. It was the future we shared, child, not a village romance. But it was love."

"Keefe says they are moving to Arbor Hill someday."

"So they may. Kevin has his own drayage company now. He has offered your da a job many's the time."

"Da likes being an officer, Ma, he says. We'll have a big house, too, someday. Senator Phelan says . . . "

"I know all about what the senator says," her mother interrupted. "We'll have to wait and see, won't we? No matter what, it's a better life here than I would have had in the village at home. Thirty years old I was with no man and people already looking sideways at me like I was an old woman. 'Too good to marry a county man,' they said. As if there were county men calling at my door by the dozen."

Ma was a fine-looking woman, Connor knew, even now with gray in her hair and worry wrinkles around her eyes. There wasn't a more beautiful woman in the parish, Da told Connor proudly. "There must have been someone who loved you, Ma," she argued.

"There was, girl. The someone was a widow man, bent over from working a poor patch of land. A poor man in a poor county in a poor country that wasn't even our country. It was a British country with British soldiers on patrol in Irish streets and British lords in Irish castles and British landlords telling Irish farmers what to do. When the letter came from Peg with the passage I was the first one on the boat."

After awhile, Ma didn't talk so much about the old country. She was proud to be an American, she told Connor, and there was no point in looking back.

Connor heard her father moving around in the bedroom. On Saturdays, he took his own sweet time, he said, when the assembly wasn't meeting. Some Saturdays he took the day off altogether, and they would go down to the Hudson River when the weather was fine and eat outside at a restaurant and watch the boats sail by.

Today was different. Da came into the kitchen in the long gray underwear he wore summer and winter, holding his jacket out to Ma. "Could you give my uniform a good press, Nora?"

"There's no fire now, Donal," Ma put her hand on the top of the stove to show him.

"Could you burn a newspaper and some of those magazines I bring home for the girl? Just warm enough for the wrinkles."

Connor's mother took some paper from the wood basket, crumpled it, and stuffed it into the stove. "Open the door," she told Connor. "And mind the smoke."

The smoldering paper sent black smoke into the room. Connor flapped a newspaper to push it out the kitchen door. When the iron was warm, Ma spread a piece of damp sheet over the jacket and smoothed away the creases. She placed the jacket across the back of a kitchen chair.

"It's an important day for me," Da announced as he slipped into his jacket. "The head woman is coming to town this evening on the train."

"Miss Anthony?" Connor asked, struggling with the damp buttons. "Susan B. Anthony?"

"The same," her father said. "And what do you know about Susan B. Anthony, lass?" he asked suspiciously.

"Sister Mary Francis told us. It's about the vote, she says, the vote for women."

"That may be what Sister Mary Francis says, but Senator Phelan and his friends say something else. I'll be home later tonight, Nora. Don't put out a plate. I'll be having my supper with the senator."

CHAPTER ELEVEN

"THE DAYS ARE GETTING LONGER," MA SAID SOFTLY. "Remember in Martinville how you could see the sun come up and the sun go down? You didn't need a clock in the kitchen to tell you the time of day."

Connor and her mother sat on the front stoop of the tenement late in the afternoon. All along the street other families were enjoying the warmth of the spring afternoon. Ma had finished the baking and scrubbing the kitchen and starting the Phelans' wash, which was spread across the lines on the porch. "We'll leave it there tonight," Ma had said. "We'll take the rest of the day off, the two of us. Your da won't be home until midnight, most likely. Later we'll walk to the Polish place and have a sausage for our supper. What do you say to that? And tomorrow we'll ask Peg and Kevin to go with us to see the park they are building on top of our old shacks in Martinville."

Her mother still longed for the shabby little house in

Martinville. What Connor remembered was the mud outside the door and Paddy nosing the heaps of garbage and the half-dressed kids who taunted her because she was a girl and wore boots all summer and sometimes had a ribbon in her hair. "Connor, Connor, she's a boy, your honor," they chanted when she came out to play. She wondered why Ma was so fond of Martinville. "Was it like your village in Ireland?" she asked.

"You mean Martinville? No, my village was a poor little place with a church and a shop and tiny white houses set along a cobbled street, with fields all around. Martinville was an awful slum. They were right to tear it down. But you were free there. You could step outside and breathe the air and hear the sounds from the river and see the stars at night. You were free." Ma paused. "I've been thinking on the words we read. I *am* a prisoner in that little place upstairs. You know that, girl, as well as I do. I see no one and talk to no one unless it's old Mrs. Dougherty at the coal bin."

"Da says we'll be moving soon."

"We'll see, lass, we'll see. I counted my wash money this morning. Eighty dollars in silver and a bit of paper money. Ten years of doing the wash from dawn to dusk and eighty dollars to show for it. Your da is welcome to it, every penny, if it will buy us a house." Ma shook her head. "But he is taking from the house money I put aside from his pay, spending it on drink again. We'll need ten times over eighty dollars, child. How much is that?"

Connor did her multiplication. As she was about to answer, her mother put a finger across her lips. "Eight hundred dollars. Am I right?" She hugged Connor close.

"It's a teacher I will be when you and the sister have finished with me."

A buggy with the top down rolled to a stop in front of the tenement. "Connor! Hey there, Connor!" a voice shouted.

"It's Doreen, it's Doreen Kruger," Connor told her mother. "What are you doing here on Canal Street?" Doreen lived in a regular house on the other side of Madison Avenue. Sometimes Connor walked her home. Doreen's ma had hot chocolate and buttered slices of bread waiting. Connor hadn't yet asked Doreen to come home with her.

"We're going to the train station. Ask your ma if she wants to come."

"I'll ask her, Doreen," Mrs. Kruger said. She stepped down from the carriage. "Would you and Connor care to come to the station with us, Mrs. O'Shea? Doreen and I have been after Mr. Kruger all day to take us to enjoy the festivity. I do believe half the city will be there."

"Please come, Ma," Connor urged. "We can tell Sister on Monday. She wanted to go, didn't she, Doreen?"

Her mother looked down at her wash dress and apron and her soap-splattered boots. "I can't be going to an occasion looking like a washerwoman, lass."

"Put on your church clothes, Ma, please. Just this once."

"Well, if Mr. and Mrs. Kruger don't mind waiting, we'd be obliged." She looked up at Mr. Kruger on the front seat of the buggy. He put the reins in his left hand and raised his derby hat.

"We'd be honored, ma'am," Mr. Kruger said. He took a

46

fat gold watch from his vest pocket. "By my calculations, the woman isn't due in town for almost an hour."

"Not 'the woman,'" Mrs. Kruger said. "Susan B. Anthony."

"Miss Anthony, then, Mother," Mr. Kruger laughed.

"I'll bring your sweater, Connor," her mother said. "It's likely to be chilly down by the river."

The flow of carriages thickened as they approached the station. "We'll stop here," Mr. Kruger said. "I noticed some boisterous young men at the station platform. They mean to make trouble."

"You mean they are drunk, Mr. Kruger," his wife said. "Irish, probably. They are a people who like their drink."

"Ma!" Doreen scolded.

"Oh, I am so sorry, Mrs. O'Shea. I let my tongue run ahead of my thoughts. Do forgive me. My father was an Irishman, William Casey, so I was speaking against my own people."

Connor's mother smiled a tight smile. She didn't speak.

"Look, Ma," Connor said. "Here come the police. Maybe we'll see Da."

Marching out of step, a column of policemen stomped two by two down the street. "The city police," Mr. Kruger announced.

Ten paces behind, eight more men marched smartly, hats set squarely, sticks held beside their thighs. One head rose above the others. "Look, Ma!" Connor almost shouted. "It *is* Da."

"The capitol police," Mr. Kruger announced. "Your father is the tall one, is he, Connor? A fine-looking man."

"Yes, sir. Shall I wave, Ma?"

Her mother touched Connor's arm. "Later, lass. We'll not want to disturb Donal at his work."

What would Da say, Connor suddenly thought, if he saw Ma and me sitting in Mr. Kruger's buggy waiting to have a look at Aunt Susan and the crazy women? He wouldn't like it much, she decided. Stay away from those women, he had warned.

A piercing light struck through the dark of evening. A steam whistle shrieked, one time, twice, and a long third time. "They're coming!" one of the drunken men bellowed. "Here come the crazy women."

CHAPTER TWELVE

THE ROWDIES, LAUGHING, SHOUTING, WAVING THEIR FISTS like the boys at St. Stephen's after school, pushed through a group of women, some of them carrying flowers, waiting on the platform. They pressed against the cars as the train came to a halt. "Where is she? Where's the crazy woman?" their leader shouted. He saw the trainman put a step stool on the platform. "It's that one, come on. That's Auntie Susan's car."

An erect gray-haired woman in spectacles stepped to the stool. Connor saw her bend over to talk to the trainman. The man shook his head. Susan B. Anthony lifted her head to stare calmly at the drunken gang. She said something else that Connor could not hear. Again the trainman shook his head, shrugged, and moved to one side. Aunt Susan, with half a dozen women from the train car close behind, stepped to the platform. The men shouted louder, ugly words that Connor could hear. Mrs. Kruger leaned forward

49

in the carriage to put her hand on her husband's shoulder. She was trembling.

Men in uniform, sticks now held high, pushed roughly through the threatening gang. "Get home with you," a harsh voice ordered the rowdies. "Go on or I'll crack your head." Connor knew the voice. "It's Da," she told her mother. "Stand up, Ma. You can see him."

"You girls stand up here with me," Mr. Kruger told Connor and Doreen. "Have a good look. It's a fine sight."

"What is the fine sight, Mr. Kruger?" his wife asked sharply. "The sight of worthless rowdies bullying a woman who has come to our city? It is a disgrace, I would say. I do not hold with Miss Anthony, but I do not wish to see her hurt."

"It's a fine show, Mother." Mr. Kruger laughed. "The heroic police have saved the women from the hooligans. Watch, the officers are escorting the women from the station. Look how pleased and polite Connor's father is. It's all part of Phelan's game, ladies."

It was Da that Mr. Kruger was talking about. What did he mean, it was part of the game?

Her mother spoke for the first time. She sounded worried and uncertain. "I do not understand, Mr. Kruger. Donal is helping Miss Anthony and the others."

"Indeed he is, Mrs. O'Shea. That is what he is supposed to do, I reckon. He works for Senator Phelan, Doreen tells me. The thing is, Mrs. O'Shea, Senator Phelan and his powerful friends don't want people in the capitol getting excited about the vote for women. There is a good deal of feeling in Albany and New York State that the convention should vote for suffrage. Mrs. Kruger and I don't hold with that view. Someday, perhaps, but not now. Government is a complicated business best left to men."

"That's not so," Doreen interrupted. "Sister says women are smarter than men. At school most of the boys can hardly write their names."

"Be that as it may"—Mr. Kruger went on, smiling—"the fact is, Doreen, women are still not smart enough to get the vote for themselves. Miss Anthony isn't as smart as Tommy Phelan. He had that gang here to frighten folks. Bought them with free beer, I'd say. Then his capitol police march in to rescue the women. Next Phelan will say—or one of the officers, most likely—that it's not safe for the women to march uptown, so Miss Anthony and her suffragists won't have the parade they were counting on. Watch."

Aunt Susan and the girls were forming lines across the center of the street. They were joined now by the other women who had been waiting at the station. The first line of women unfurled a long banner that stretched across half the line. In the dim reflection of the streetlight, Connor read, "Votes for Women."

Miss Anthony took a place in the line. She raised her hand, and the women began to march. A tall policeman approached the marchers. He lifted his hat and spoke to Aunt Susan. It was Da again, no doubt about it. He bent down to listen politely to what the gray-haired woman replied. Still smiling, he gestured toward the sidewalk where the hooligans lingered. Several of them lifted their fists and shouted insults.

Aunt Susan shook her head. She gestured back to the women, some of them carrying suitcases, others with arm-fuls of pamphlets. Then she nodded up the hill.

Da shook his head. He won't let them pass, Connor thought with disappointment. He pointed again to the young men on the pavement. He pointed to the capitol policemen, and the women with suitcases.

"He's saying his men will carry the women's luggage, but it isn't safe for them to march," Mr. Kruger explained. "That Phelan is a real smarty."

Impatiently, Miss Anthony shook her head. Again she motioned to the lines of women in back of her. She said something to Da and moved forward, the women following closely. The lines of women, now singing "Glory, Glory, Hallelujah," swept around the lonely figure of Donal O'Shea.

Da looked toward the capitol policemen for help. They moved toward the street.

"No, no, let them pass!" cried the spectators. Women and a handful of men moved into the street to join the parade.

Connor watched her father speak to the leader of the rowdies. The man shook his head. He wasn't going to break up the parade, it was clear. Da scratched his head. He looked around for someone—probably Senator Phelan, Connor thought—then disappeared into the crowd.

"First score for Susan B. Anthony," said Mr. Kruger. "It serves Senator Phelan right. Fair play, I say. She's a straight-minded woman, ladies, I'll say that for her. It looks like the party is over. Let's join the parade." He slapped the reins lightly and turned the carriage to follow the marching women.

CHAPTER THIRTEEN

In the middle of the night Connor heard the door to her room open and quietly close. Her mother crept into her bed and put her arms around her daughter. Connor could feel Ma shake with sobbing. "Ma? What's wrong, Ma?" she whispered.

"Shh," Ma said and put her hand over Connor's mouth.

On the other side of the wall Connor heard a thump, then another. Da was pulling off his boots. A shout, "Nora, come here, woman!" was followed by a lot of swearing. The springs creaked as Da collapsed on the bed. Soon Connor heard his familiar snore. She took her mother's hand and held it tight.

Ma was gone when Connor awoke in her windowless room. The washed sheets hung around her bed like shrouds. She remembered that she and her mother had brought them in from the porch when they returned from the station. There had been lightning in the sky, and Mr.

Kruger had said there was a thunderstorm on the way. Connor reached out to touch the heavy muslin sheets from the servants' beds. They were damp and coarse, not like the fine silky cottons from the Phelans' bed.

Where was Ma? And Da? Carefully Connor stood up and listened. Not a sound from the bedroom, not a sound from the kitchen. It must be time to get up for church. She opened her door and slipped out into the hallway.

Ma was sitting at the kitchen table in her Sunday dress and button shoes, staring down at the flowered bonnet in her lap. When Connor approached she looked up. Connor saw that one side of Ma's face was purple and black. Ma took a cloth from the table to hold to her face. She smiled a sad one-sided smile. "Get yourself dressed, child, and we'll go along to church. Then we'll make a day of it, the two of us."

"What about Da?" Connor asked in a low voice.

"We'll let him sleep. Then he'll be off to the capitol again, I should think."

"Peg and Kevin, they're coming to tea, you remember, Ma?"

"I don't believe they'll be coming. Your father talked to them last night."

They must have been at the station, too, to see the crazy women, Connor thought. They must have been across the street in the crowd where Da was. She went to her room and took her best dress and the brown, laced shoes from the tiny wardrobe. Her sweater was folded neatly at the foot of her bed. Ma would take a ribbon from the sewing drawer for her hair.

Her mother didn't talk on the way to church. During the

54

Mass she stared straight ahead to the altar. Connor had never felt her mother so far away. She slipped her hand into Ma's gloved hand. "It's all right, Ma," she whispered. "Please, it's all right." Her mother nodded that she had heard.

Outside, Ma spoke for the first time. "We'll have a look first for Paddy and see how the new park is coming along. Then we'll go up to Washington Park. They'll be selling treats. I brought a dollar from the wash money for us." She patted her dress pocket.

The last of the rickety buildings in Martinville had been torn down. Connor studied the ground, puzzling over where the shack had been. It hadn't been far from Buttermilk Falls where the Beaverkill tumbled into a churning pool. "It was about here, wasn't it, Ma?" she asked. "There were the tenements in back, between us and the falls."

"Aye," her mother agreed. "It was the place next to Kevin and Peg's little house. You don't remember. They moved soon after you were born. Your da and I went straight from our wedding to the party at their house." Ma's eyes grew teary. "It was a fine party. We had music and dancing and the men took too much to drink and the women had to lead them home." She sighed. "Well, the party's over now, isn't it, girl? Where do you suppose Paddy found a home? He was a funny beast, he was. Sometimes he took it into his mind that he wanted inside. He'd stand at the door and butt it with his head until you opened it for him."

"He never stayed," Connor said. "He'd have a look around and decide he wanted out. Da said goats were crazy, but smart. Paddy could look after himself, Da said, when we moved."

"Better than humans, at any rate. Let's be off. Beaver Park they'll be calling it here, you say?"

"Beaver or Lincoln, Sister said. They haven't decided. Ma?" Connor pointed to the swollen cheek. "Da did your face like that?"

Connor's mother nodded.

"He was drunk again, was he? I didn't hear." Usually Da spoke in a loud voice when he threatened her mother.

"He said Kevin told him we were at the station."

"But, Ma, it was Doreen's parents who asked us. That was all right."

"Your father had it in his head that he told you to stay away from the crazy women. He said he had promised to strap you if you didn't mind."

"That was for talking to Bertha, that was all. And taking the pamphlet."

"You hadn't told me, Connor, what Da said to you. But it doesn't matter. I decided a long time ago he wasn't going to do that again ever. That's what I told him, clear as a bell. You'll not be strapping my daughter, Donal. Not now, not ever."

"It doesn't matter, Ma. It only hurts a little. It's only just a couple of licks."

"I took the strap from his hand. That was when he struck my face. Drunk as he was, he fell to the floor. I left him there. Let's get up to the park, lassie. We'll have cakes and lemonade."

56

CHAPTER FOURTEEN

HUNDREDS OF PEOPLE WERE ENJOYING THE WARMTH OF a pleasant Sunday. Men in their dark Sunday suits and women with their parasols strolled along the paths, keeping an eye on their children playing on the grass. Old people sat on the iron benches in the sunshine, some of them unfolding the butcher paper around their lunch. Boys ran down the hillside trying to raise kites made of newspaper into the breeze. Here and there Connor noticed Aunt Susan's girls in their red-ribboned bonnets, passing out pamphlets.

"We'll sit here on the grass," Connor's mother said. She put her hand to the ground. "It's nice and dry." She handed Connor a silver dollar. "Get us two little cakes and lemonade. You may use what's left for yourself."

"Vanilla or strawberry frosting?" Connor asked.

Ma put two fingers to her lips the way she did when she

was considering what to say. "What did I have last time when we were here with Da?"

That had been in the autumn, Connor recalled, when the leaves on the trees in Washington Park were turning red and gold. Da brought the cakes and lemonade to Connor and Ma seated on a bench. It was a strawberry cake he had brought, she decided. "Strawberry," she said.

"Today I'll have vanilla, thank you," Ma said, trying again to smile. She put her hand to her face. "Is it swollen real bad?"

"It looks fine, Ma. Not swollen much at all, I'd say. I'll get some ice in my handkerchief to put on it."

Connor made her way to the refreshment cart. A man in a straw hat and a red-and-white striped jacket was hawking ice creams and drinks and pastries beneath a red-and-white awning. "What will you have, miss? Italian ices, French pastry, American lemonade, we have the best."

"One of those." Connor pointed to a square vanilla pastry. "And one of those," pointing to a chocolate puff. "How much is that?"

"Thirty cents."

"Two lemonades with cherries."

"Twenty cents. Half a dollar altogether."

"And some ice here in my handkerchief, please."

"The ice is free," the man said. "Here you are, miss. And your change, fifty cents."

I'll save it, thought Connor. I'll put it in the cough drop tin Doreen gave me, with the pennies I have saved. Someday when Da is the captain and we're ready to buy the house, I can help, too. Not for much, but for something we'll be needing in the house.

"It's you, Connor, is it?" she heard a familiar pleasant voice ask.

Bertha was standing behind her next to a tall, stern-looking old woman. Bertha's mother? Or grandmother? Connor wondered. No, she realized, the woman was Aunt Susan, Miss Anthony. Bertha was saying, "This is Connor, Connor O'Shea. She took three booklets last week. She was my best customer. I promised you I'd tell her, didn't I, Connor?"

"Yes, miss," Connor mumbled. "I gave one to my teacher. She explained some of it to my friend and me."

The stern countenance behind the wire-rimmed glasses relaxed into a smile. "And what did you find out, Connor?"

"That it's not right, Sister said, for men to vote and women not to be allowed to. They both live in the same democracy, she said."

"That's what the sister said, Connor. I'd like to know what *you* think. And your friend. What's her name?"

"Doreen, Doreen Kruger. She agrees with Sister. So do I." I do agree, Connor told herself. It was no lie. She wasn't so sure about Doreen. It wasn't right that Ma couldn't vote if she wanted to. Someday she could go with Ma to the voting place, maybe with Da, too, if he practiced his reading, and vote for Senator Phelan if he decided to be the governor. But maybe they wouldn't. Maybe they wouldn't if the senator was to stand against the vote for women. Connor heard Bertha say something. "Yes, miss? I'm sorry. Ma says I daydream too much."

"I said Aunt Susan and I would like to meet your mother. Is she here with your father?"

"Only Ma. Da is working today." She'd better not say

where he was working and that it was her father who last night tried to keep Susan B. Anthony and her friends from having a parade uptown from the station. "My mother is over there on the grass. We're having a Sunday treat."

"Let me help you," Bertha said. "I'll take the lemonade."

"Wait a minute, miss," Connor said. If Susan B. Anthony and Bertha were going to meet her mother, the first thing Ma would do would be to give them the lemonades. To be polite, Ma would explain to Connor afterward.

Connor turned to the refreshment man. "Give me two more lemonades," she said.

"My mother is over there," Connor told the women, leading the way. "She hurt her face. I have some ice to put on it." Now Ma won't have to explain, Connor thought. Bertha and Aunt Susan were bound to be surprised when they saw the awful bruise.

CHAPTER FIFTEEN

CONNOR TRIED TO KEEP THE EXCITEMENT OUT OF HER voice. "Ma, I met Bertha at the refreshment cart. You know, Bertha, she's the woman I told you about. And Aunt Susan's with her—Miss Anthony, I mean. I bought two lemonades for them. Was that all right? They can have my puff," she whispered.

"Mrs. O'Shea," Bertha said, "I have your lemonade, Connor's too."

"Those are for you and Miss Anthony," Connor replied. "I have ours. And there's a chocolate puff here you both can have. Do you like chocolate?"

"It's my favorite," Susan B. Anthony said. She knelt on the grass. "May we join you, Mrs. O'Shea? I confess my legs are not as strong as they used to be."

"Don't you believe her," Bertha said. "Two weeks ago I saw her parade practically from one end of Manhattan Island to the other. She put us younger women to shame."

"There's a bench over there," Connor's mother said. "You would be more comfortable."

"The grass is fine," Aunt Susan said. She took a bite of Connor's puff and handed it to Bertha. "Your half, Bertha. It will keep you going until teatime."

Ma didn't know what to say, Connor could see. She would be all right if Connor could get her started. "I told Miss Anthony and Bertha we saw the parade last night."

"I'm sorry for the trouble you had," her mother said. "It was a sorry welcome to the city."

"I can't say I've ever had a very warm welcome in Albany, Mrs. O'Shea. It is a city run by powerful, ignorant men. The reception was rather what we had expected. But we have to show our faces in the capital to let people know we are here." Susan B. Anthony smiled.

She wasn't so stern, after all, Connor decided. "Do you like the lemonade?" she asked.

"It's very good," Bertha replied. "Tell them about the reception in Rochester, Aunt Susan."

Miss Anthony laughed outright. "That's my hometown," she explained. "I guess it's my hometown. It's not where I was born, but it's the place I keep going back to. Last month the suffragists held a parade there. Quite a number of local women participated. The people against us, men and women both, decided to have a parade at the same time."

"The other marchers carried signs," Bertha said. "Signs saying, 'Susan B. Anthony, go home,' can you imagine? There wasn't room for the two parades to pass each other on the street, so Aunt Susan went up to some of the women and told them they should turn around and join *our* parade. 'You'll get the vote sooner if you join us now instead of later,' she said. And would you believe it, maybe ten or twelve women did turn around to march with us, leaving their husbands standing there looking surprised. I believe one of them came along with his wife, didn't he?"

"Yes," Miss Anthony said. "Of course it didn't do much good, but once in a while you find encouragement. Are you interested in the vote for women, Mrs. O'Shea?"

Her mother was confused by such a direct question. Connor held out the handkerchief with the ice in it. "Put this on your cheek, Ma. It will help." Maybe if Ma did that, she wouldn't have to reply.

Ma shook her head. "Later, lass." Very firmly she spoke to Susan Anthony. "I believe I am. I was born and raised in Ireland where none of us, man or woman, had a vote. And I have lived here for fifteen years without rightly knowing what a vote was. Now the sister has explained it to my daughter and she has explained it to me and"—Ma paused—"well, now it seems right to me. This is my country and I believe I should have a say in its business if I want to."

Embarrassed at having said so much, she put her head down to stare at the melting ice in her lap.

"Bravo!" Bertha said. "I have never heard it said better, Mrs. O'Shea. We have a convert, Aunt Susan."

Miss Anthony had taken off her glasses and was dabbing a handkerchief at her eyes. "I must be honest, Mrs. O'Shea. We are not going to get the vote in Albany this year, and probably not in Kansas, either. But we will someday, I promise you we will. We have freed the slaves in this country, though it took a civil war, and we will free the women too."

63

Bertha opened a gold watch hanging from a gold chain around her neck. "It's one o'clock," she said gently. "Time for you to talk to the ladies." She stood up and put out her hand to Aunt Susan. "We have a talk scheduled at the bandstand," she told Connor and her mother. "Would you like to come along?"

The firemen's band had played the last march. The firemen put their instruments in cases and stepped down. Two women draped the sides of the bandstand with red, white, and blue bunting. A large middle-aged woman with papers in her hand stood at the railing watching people gather.

"That's the governor's wife," Bertha said. "She's for us. So is the governor, but he won't come straight out and say so. He's afraid of Senator Phelan."

A crowd of women, hundreds it seemed to Connor, and a handful of men gathered around the bandstand. "Come closer, Ma," Connor urged. "So we can hear."

Susan B. Anthony joined the governor's wife. She listened politely to a flowery introduction and the applause from the crowd. She approached the railing, held it firmly with her two hands, and faced the crowd. "I came here," she began, "many years ago, to help persuade the convention to vote for woman suffrage. The men at the convention did not so vote. I have returned here in 1894 to tell the men of New York State to right that wrong this time. The governor of the state says he endorses our petition. A majority of women and, in their hearts I believe, a majority of men voters support us."

Aunt Susan stopped, it seemed to Connor, to gather her strength. "We have been denied representation at the convention. I am here to persuade the politicians of both parties to hear us out, to open their minds to our petition. I understand to my sorrow that woman's rights in New York face defeat again. But let me tell you that I will return; so long as I live I will return. And others will follow me when I am gone. Women will prevail. What we say is right and fair and we will prevail. I urge you all please to support us in our struggle for suffrage for women."

CHAPTER SIXTEEN

"Let us be going home," Ma said. "The women have their business to attend to. It was a fine speech, Connor. It made me proud to be living in this country where a woman can get up and say what's on her mind. She's a fine woman, Susan B. Anthony."

"Bertha, too, Ma. Miss Anthony counts on her a lot."

"So she must. They are both women for getting things done, you can see."

"Like Sister Mary Francis," Connor added.

"Like Sister Mary Francis," Ma echoed. She gave Connor a crooked smile. "Does it make you feel good to be a woman, lass, and not a fresh boy like your cousin Keefe getting muddy pushing other boys down into the Beaverkill?"

"I guess." Connor hadn't thought much about being a boy the last couple of days. She remembered that Sister always said it was the girls she went to when she wanted something done properly.

On the path ahead she noticed a familiar figure staring at Ma and her. It was Senator Phelan, his wife holding his arm. The senator lifted his derby. He smiled at Connor. Why, he's no taller than I am, Connor noticed. He's not even as tall as his wife, who nodded briefly.

"A splendid day, Connor, is it not?" the senator said. "I don't believe I have had the pleasure of meeting you, Mrs. O'Shea. You have been to listen to our famous visitor?"

"Yes," Connor answered for Ma and herself.

"A powerful speaker, Susan B. Anthony." Senator Phelan continued, still smiling, "Not like our men in the assembly who would drone on until midnight if Donal and I allowed them. Miss Anthony spoke straight to the point, did she not? She is a woman to be reckoned with. Mrs. Phelan was much impressed, although she is not of Miss Anthony's persuasion." Senator Phelan lifted his hat again. "Ladies," he said. He and Mrs. Phelan walked on.

"I guess I know my place," Connor's mother said bitterly.

"Why is that, Ma? Senator Phelan spoke to you. He's always nice to me."

"Yes, he did, and he tipped his hat. I will say that for your da's friend, he has fine manners. It was the senator's wife I was talking about. Never a word of greeting for her washerwoman when she meets her in the public park."

"But, Ma, she talks to you on Fridays."

"Indeed she does. She says thank you when she hands me four paper dollars and has her maid bring my daughter a piece of rock candy. A fine lady, our Mrs. Phelan. Come along now, Connor, we'll see if your da is home."

Her father was slumped over the kitchen table, his head on his arms. An empty whiskey bottle lay on its side. At the sound of their entrance, he lurched back in his chair. His head rolling from side to side, he stared at them with bloodshot eyes. Half the buttons on his police jacket were undone. It was soiled and smelled sour.

Ma passed by the table without a word. She pushed the back door out as wide as it would go and wedged it open. She put her arm around Connor. "Let us go into the parlor, lass. I'll make us a pot of tea and buttered bread for our supper."

Da pushed himself to his feet. "The girl stays here," he growled. He glared at Connor. "You and your fancy friends saw your old da made a fool of in front of half the city. What do you say to that, Connor O'Shea, your father acting the fool?" He slumped back into his chair. "I told you to stay away from those crazy women. They have brought disgrace to your old da, and my girl was there to see it."

He reached for the empty bottle. He put it to his mouth, then let it drop to the floor. "Skip down to the Black Shamrock, lass, for a bucket of beer. Tell Mike I'll bring the bucket and the money by tomorrow."

"It's Sunday, Donal," her mother said firmly. "There will be no beer on Sunday, unless they go against the law. Get out of your jacket and I will try to clean it for you. Give him a hand with the buttons, Connor."

Holding her breath against the smell, Connor undid the bottom buttons. Da pulled one sleeve free, then the other.

The jacket fell to the floor. Ma picked it up and spread it across the other end of the table. She scrubbed the front of the jacket with a soapy cloth. "Get me the ammonia bottle," she told Connor, "and get the fire started. We'll have our supper in the kitchen. We'll all be needing some proper food." Ignoring her husband, she bent over the jacket.

Her father poured some tea into his saucer. He lifted it to his mouth and blew. "Senator Phelan said I was a fool, Nora," he said morosely. "They made a fool of me. 'An important job, Donal,' he said. 'I trusted you. I gave you an important job and you acted the fool.'"

"Did he give you a bottle of whiskey for being the fool?" Ma asked.

"That was Conlan who gave me the bottle, feeling sorry for me, he was. He keeps a bottle in his locker at the capitol. He was there on duty this morning. Jocko heard it all. Afterward he slipped me the bottle. 'You'll be needing this, Donal,' he said."

"Senator Phelan was at the capitol, was he?" Ma asked. She didn't say that she and Connor had seen him in Washington Park.

"He was there right enough. There waiting for me, and I was late. 'Right after church,' he told me last night, 'I want you in my office right after church.' He shouted at me, Nora, called me an idiot and a fool."

"Why was that, Donal?"

"You and the girl saw why. So did the others. That woman, that crazy old woman who ought to be home next to the stove, Susan B. Anthony, she marched past me with her women like I was a piece of dirt."

"They just wanted to parade uptown, Da," Connor interrupted. "That was all they wanted, to parade so people would know they wanted the vote."

Her father fixed Connor with a wicked smile. He made a fist in front of Connor's face. "You! I told you once and I'll tell you again, girl. You keep away from these women. They are witches, every living one of them. I still have my strap around my waist and I will use it on you, so help me, God. And your ma too," he threatened, "if she tries to stop me."

Connor's mother paid no attention to Da's words. "Why were you a fool, Donal?" she asked again calmly.

"The senator told me to put a stop to any parades or demonstrations. That was my job. The senator got some of the boys in the saloon drunk and excited and headed them down to the station for when the train came in."

"Where you and your men were to save Miss Anthony and her friends and show them to their boardinghouses or wherever they would be lodging. Is that correct?"

"That was the plan."

"Mr. Kruger told us that. He said it was a sham."

"She wouldn't listen to me," Da said sadly. "I told her the men were drunk and dangerous, that we couldn't protect her from the crowd. I told her everything the senator told me to tell her."

"And she paid you no mind, Donal?" Ma asked. A quick smile flashed across her face.

"She made a fool of me and my men. 'What was I to do?' I asked Senator Phelan. 'A permit, Donal,' he replied. 'If Susan B. Anthony didn't listen, you were supposed to have enough wits in your head to tell her they couldn't have a parade without a permit. You know what a permit is, don't you, Donal?' 'But you didn't tell me about a permit,' I said. That was when he said a man who hoped to be captain of the capitol police ought to know about permits and the like."

Ma was silent. She polished the buttons on the police jacket with the dish towel.

Da got to his feet. "I'll get it back," he said in a hard voice. "I'll get it back from those crazy women and their Susan B. Anthony. You mind my words, Nora. I'll get it back." He stumbled toward the bedroom.

Connor watched him go. Not a word, she thought, not a single word about Ma's face. Da wasn't even sorry.

CHAPTER SEVENTEEN

SISTER MARY M. STOOD AT THE GIRLS' DOOR MONDAY morning shaking the bell angrily at Connor and Doreen as they scurried across the schoolyard. "Hurry along, you two. You're always the last ones in." Sister scowled to show them she was dead serious. "If you can't be on time you'll never be allowed to enter the convent. Obedience, that's the first thing they teach us, obedience."

"Who said anything about entering the convent?" Doreen whispered. "My father says I am going to a women's college. That's the way for me to get ahead, he tells my mother, not by going to the voting place." She slid into her seat and put her clasped hands on the top of her desk, the way the girls were supposed to until the first class began.

Sister Mary Francis came down the aisle. She handed Connor an envelope. "For you," she said bending over.

"Don't open it until recess. Miss Hall brought it along early."

Connor turned the envelope over. It was made of thick pale blue paper. It had a faint scent of perfume like the scents that floated from the carriages on their way to Arbor Hill in the afternoon. Her name, Miss Connor O'Shea, was written in a beautiful hand on the front. Puzzled, Connor passed the envelope under her desk to Doreen who was waiting anxiously.

Doreen studied the writing and smelled the envelope. "Who?" she formed on her lips.

Connor shrugged. Up front Sister Mary Francis was saying, "We'll start our reading now if Connor and Doreen are ready." The other girls giggled. The sister began to tell them about Washington Irving, who wrote stories about the Hudson River country. "Have you all read *The Legend of Sleepy Hollow?*" she asked.

Doreen raised her hand before Connor, whose thoughts were on the mysterious letter, could raise hers. She didn't know anyone named Miss Hall. And she certainly didn't know anyone who would leave a letter for her at the schoolhouse. In fact the only women she knew outside of school were Ma and Peg and Mrs. Phelan. And old Mrs. Dougherty on the second floor.

"Open it quick, Connor," Doreen ordered when the class was dismissed for morning recess. "Who's it from, do you know?"

Connor shook her head. Carefully, so as not to tear it, she lifted the flap. She took out a folded piece of paper the same color as the envelope. The scent was stronger.

Lavender. "Dear Connor," the note read. "Would you and some of your friends like to help Aunt Susan and me after school? We need helpers to sort pamphlets and put them in envelopes and deliver them to the homes of women on our list. We can't pay, but we'll provide an elegant tea. Tell me what you decide on your way home. I'll be on my favorite corner waiting for you. Bertha Hall."

So Miss Hall was her friend Bertha. Why hadn't she figured it out? Connor wondered. Bertha was the only other woman she knew. "Would you want to, Doreen?" she asked. "Would your mother let you?"

"How about yours?" Doreen replied.

"Maybe. On the days when I don't have to take the wash. Let's talk to Sister after school."

"I can't advise you," Sister Mary Francis said. "It's for your parents to say. It would be nice, though. I wish I could. What Susan B. Anthony and her women are doing is very important, helping women to become equal citizens in this country. Someday you might want to remember that you helped out."

"Let's ask your mother first," Connor suggested. She had a feeling Ma would say yes if Doreen's folks had agreed.

"She'll have to ask my father," Doreen said. "Mom does what he says. What about you, Connor? *Your* father is a policeman."

Connor couldn't say that Da would lock her in her room to keep her from helping the crazy women, especially Susan B. Anthony, who had made him look the fool. "Ma can give me permission," she replied.

Mrs. Kruger had hot chocolate and cinnamon buns waiting. She read Bertha Hall's letter and listened patiently while Doreen explained what Sister Mary Francis had said. "I wonder if this is the same Hall family that lives at the top of Arbor Hill," Mrs. Kruger said, half to herself. "They may be one of the richest families in Albany. There was some tragedy in the family, I seem to recall. Well, your father won't say no to *them*. Why don't you walk down to Swan Street with Connor and find out where you'll be going? Your father and I would like to know."

Bertha was standing right where she had promised. Connor looked toward the capitol steps. Da wasn't in sight. She turned her back to the building. "We have to find out where you live," she said. "And how much time you'll need us for. I have to help my mother some afternoons."

"It's on Arbor Hill," Bertha said. "Not too far from your school if you come along the side streets. You will be there the rest of the afternoon, I suppose, until it begins to get dark. What you do will depend on what the women want. You'll have a tea and maybe an early supper. What about your homework?"

"That will be all right," Doreen assured Bertha. "Sister will be easy on us when we tell her we're helping Miss Anthony."

"Would she like to come along, too?" Bertha asked. "We need everyone we can find. They have agreed now to let Aunt Susan and some other suffragists address the delegation. We want to have a lot of women at the capitol."

"She can't," Connor said. "Nuns aren't supposed to do outside things."

"That's a pity," Bertha said. "Anyway, see what your parents say. I'll come up Madison Avenue tomorrow afternoon to meet you. I don't do much business on this corner, I tell

75

Aunt Susan. But she says we have to make a show. Do you have any other friends?"

Connor looked at Doreen. "I don't think so," she explained. "Most of the girls have to help their mothers after school."

CHAPTER EIGHTEEN

CONNOR'S MOTHER SET THE IRON ON THE STOVE AND took a seat at the table. "Now, start over again, lass, and tell me slowly what you want to do."

"Bertha, you remember her from yesterday—her full name is Bertha Hall, and Mrs. Kruger said she wouldn't be surprised if she weren't from a rich family on Arbor Hill— asked Doreen and me—me, really, and I asked Doreen—if we would come to her house where Aunt Susan and some suffrage women are working and help out with odd jobs and the like."

"Tell me the rest of it, Connor."

"There isn't any rest of it, Ma. It's sorting stuff out, Bertha said, and delivering letters and pamphlets to important women in Albany about the convention and what they can do for the vote. Oh, and the men who are running the convention, they are going to let Aunt Susan talk, Bertha said, but she can't be part of the delegation that does the deciding. They are all men. There are a lot of clergymen and bankers in New York City who don't want to share suffrage, Bertha told Doreen and me."

"So the men won't let the women vote to have the vote," Ma said to herself. "I suppose that makes some sort of sense. But they are going to let them talk, for whatever talk is worth. It sounds to me like your da's friend Senator Phelan has his finger in the pie somewhere."

"Can I go, Ma?" Connor asked impatiently. "Please, Ma." For the first time since she had come into the kitchen, Connor had a careful look at Ma's face. The swelling had gone down since yesterday, but the bruise was turning an ugly shade of yellow.

"And who will tell your da, child?"

Connor had thought of her father's threats all the way home. No matter what her mother said about his not taking the strap to her, Connor knew that Da would if he found out she was helping the crazy women. If Ma tried to stop him he'd be sure to punch her again. He'd have to, just to show Ma and her that what he said was the law and they had better mind.

"I don't know, Ma, I don't want to cause any more trouble. But it doesn't seem right that I can't help Bertha and her friends if I want to. It's not like Doreen and I are going to vote or anything. Doreen's mother and father are both against suffrage for women, too, just like Da."

"You really want to do it?" her mother asked. "And you think the Krugers will let Doreen go along?"

"It sounds like it. Doreen gets her way most of the time."

"Do you think you could be home before Da gets here?

If you were late once, I could say you were out delivering some shirts. But only once or twice, mind you."

Ma was going to say yes. It wouldn't be for long, she thought. It sounded like the convention was going to decide pretty soon; that was why the suffragists wanted Doreen and her. Until then, Da would probably be at the capitol late every night with Senator Phelan. "I'll be home before dark, Ma. They're going to give us a tea late in the afternoon. I'll be home by six-thirty. Da's never here before seven."

Ma gave Connor a crooked smile. "Then you must do it. That's what my ma said when Peg sent me the money for the passage. 'You must do it if your heart is set,' she told me. 'You must get up and out when you have the chance. There's no good life here for you, Nora. You'll just grow old like Da and me.' So let's not worry, Connor, you and me, about what your da thinks. Sometimes he's not thinking for himself at all. He's only doing what Senator Phelan tells him."

Ma stood up and reached for the iron. "Connor," she said softly, then paused.

"Yes, Ma, what is it?"

"I was thinking while you were talking, just thinking, mind you, that I could help, too, one or two afternoons when I was done with the clothes. Your Bertha said they needed whatever help they could get. Could you keep your eye out if there is something I could do, like the dishes, maybe, or preparing the tea? It seems like good work Miss Anthony is doing. I think I would like to help."

"Oh, Ma," Connor cried. "You bet I will. Give me a day or two to find out. I'll ask Miss Susan B. Anthony straight if my mother can do something. She'll say yes, I know she will."

"Don't hurry her, child. You figure it out for yourself before you say anything. Now take these shirts up to the capitol. Your da forgot them, he was in such a hurry this morning. They're for one of the assemblymen. He knows which one."

"My father said yes!" Doreen shouted halfway across Madison Avenue in the morning. She dodged among the horse carts to join Connor on the pavement. "He said he couldn't agree with Miss Anthony, but that it was time I learned to do some things on my own. I'll be going off to college someday all by myself, like Sister Mary Francis."

Connor felt the loneliness come over her the way it always did when Doreen talked about going away. For next year Doreen's parents were talking about sending her to Miss Pugh's Academy for Girls. And after next year Connor knew *she* would be finished with her schooling. That was the age when most of the girls at St. Stephen's went out to find work. They were talking about it already. Jobs in the bakery or the shoe factory or, if you were lucky, as a shop assistant downtown.

I won't think about it now, Connor persuaded herself. Right now we're going up to Arbor Hill to help Aunt Susan and the crazy women. Next year or the next one after that when Da gets to be captain of the capitol police, I will think about it then.

80

CHAPTER NINETEEN

"IT'S NEAR THE TOP OF THE HILL," BERTHA HALL TOLD Connor and Doreen. "On Ten Broeck Street."

"Ten Broeck?" Doreen exclaimed. "Millionaire's Row? That's what my father calls it. We take carriage rides some Sunday afternoons to Arbor Hill. My mother likes to look at the fancy houses."

"It used to be pretty fancy, I guess," Bertha said. "I'm not so sure it is now. Most people would rather live along Washington Park, I believe. Ten Broeck is a lonely street. I can't truthfully say I know anyone there, not even the families next door."

They turned from Northern Boulevard onto Ten Broeck Street. Connor had never been to this section of Arbor Hill. Senator Phelan lived on Pearl Street in a big house—at least it looked pretty big from the back—but the houses they were walking past now were far grander than anything she had ever seen, great brown palaces with funny turrets and narrow windows and thin chimneys poking out of slate roofs, each house as dark and brooding, it seemed to her, as the one next door. She wasn't at all sure now that Arbor Hill was where she would like to live.

"Well, here we are," Bertha said. "Pretty grim, isn't it? It's not so bad inside, especially with the suffrage women visiting."

They had come to the corner of Hall and Ten Broeck. The mansion was larger than any of the ones they had passed, as large as the capitol. Bertha's father must really be rich, Connor decided, not rich like the Phelans but rich like the Van Rensselaers or the Olcotts that Da talked about sometimes. What would he say when she told him about where Bertha Hall lived? She cut the thought short. She mustn't say a word. She'd have to watch her tongue every minute or she would never come back to Ten Broeck Street.

"I remember this house," Connor heard Doreen tell Bertha. "My father said it just might be the biggest in the city. We tried to guess how many rooms it had."

"I'm sorry I can't tell you." Bertha laughed. "I don't think I ever counted them. You tell your father that most of the rooms are cold and dusty and empty. It's an ugly place, really. All these houses along here are like big brown dinosaurs, and you both know what happened to them. I'm thinking of putting the place up for sale. I'm not sure I'll find a buyer."

"It's yours, altogether yours?" Doreen asked in disbelief. "Where are your parents?"

"They're gone, Doreen. They both drowned. Remember the excursion boat, the *Albany Queen*?"

Connor remembered, barely. A long time ago, when they

were living in Martinville, Da was working at the tannery and had spent a night and all the next day, he used to tell her, bringing the bodies ashore. "It was to see the fireworks, along the shore," he explained. "The ship filled up with people and took them out onto the Hudson where they could have refreshments and see the fireworks on the Fourth of July. There were too many people on the top deck and all of a sudden they were of a mind, all of them, to rush to one side. The *Albany Queen* turned over easy as you please. One minute she was out there all lighted up, the next minute she was upside down, just like this." Da turned his empty teacup over in his hand. "Hundreds of people were drowned. They kept bringing them ashore for days."

"My da told me," Connor said. Maybe she ought not to tell Bertha exactly what Da had told her.

"I was almost on the boat," Bertha said sadly, "but my aunt took me to a picnic instead. Afterward Aunt Catherine came here to look after me. Well, let's go see what the women are up to and what jobs we can find for you."

Inside, the great house was bright and busy. Women were walking from room to room, many of them in their red-ribboned bonnets. Others were moving up and down the carpeted stairway and working at a huge table in what Connor guessed was the dining room.

"We'll tell Aunt Catherine we're here," Bertha said. "She'll be in the kitchen."

A tall gray-haired woman who looked a lot like Bertha was talking to two women, one old and one young, who were dressed like the maids that Connor saw at the Phelans' house.

The tall woman smiled at Connor and Doreen and

kissed Bertha on the cheek. "So you're home, are you? I'm trying to get things straightened out here. There are simply too many people in the house for Martha and Bessie to take care of. Martha is threatening to leave us, but I don't believe she will. Am I right, Martha?"

"I don't know, Miss Catherine. When it's just you and Miss Bertha and the stray visitor, Bessie and I can take care of you *and* the house, with Mike doing the yard and the heavy jobs. We can't keep up now, we can't, even if we go day and night."

"It's only for two more weeks, Martha," Bertha said. "They're going to take the vote at the convention in a fortnight, and everyone, almost everyone, will be gone after that. Can you keep going for two weeks?"

"I don't know, miss. We'll try, won't we, Bessie? If you could find us some help, we'd be obliged."

"I've tried, I've looked everywhere," the tall woman explained. "You just can't reach out and pick someone worthwhile these days. Women would rather work downtown in the shops, even in the mills, than do domestic service."

"Hold on, Martha, hold on for a little longer," Bertha said. "Come with me, girls, we'll go see Aunt Susan."

Connor tugged at Bertha's sleeve when they'd left the kitchen. She might as well ask about Ma now. Aunt Catherine looked pretty desperate. "Bertha, I mean Miss Hall, I—"

"Bertha it is, Connor."

"We didn't know your last name before, did we, Connor?" said Doreen.

"No matter, I'm still Bertha."

"My mother said if there was anything she could do to help out, I was to ask you. Not for pay, I mean, just to help out. She can come some afternoons, she said, when she gets the wash done. Not Fridays, though, me, either, unless"— Connor thought ahead—"unless we could take Mrs. Phelan's wash to her on the way. We could do that, maybe."

"Do you think she could help Martha for a while, Connor? It would be a tremendous help. We'd have to pay, you understand. We couldn't accept her help for nothing."

"She wouldn't come," Connor said firmly. "Ma's not false proud, you understand, and she'll work at whatever there is to be done, but I think she'd want to be like the others. You don't pay them, do you?"

"I understand, Connor. I'm sorry I offered. No, Aunt Susan doesn't pay them. They are here because it's important. They have left their homes and, in some cases, their employment, to come to Albany until the convention decides. You can tell your mother that. She'll have our gratitude."

"I'll tell her," Connor said. "She'll like that, I think."

CHAPTER TWENTY

"BERTHA TOOK US TO SEE MISS ANTHONY," CONNOR told her mother. She trimmed the fat from the slice of meat Ma had put on her plate along with a cold cooked potato and a spoonful of warm beans.

"We'll not be waiting for your da these nights," her mother had told her. "He'll come along when he's ready."

"She—Miss Anthony—was in the room Bertha called the library. There were books on shelves all the way from the floor to the ceiling. You never saw so many. Bertha said we could borrow any we were interested in. And the floor, Ma. I forgot about the floor. It was shiny marble, pink and gray. There were these big, colored carpets, some with flowers and some with squares and figures."

"Persian rugs they must have been, like ones I saw at Swithenbanks when I bought the piece of carpet for the parlor. The prices took my breath away. Handmade, all of them, in faraway places. What was Susan B. Anthony doing?"

"Writing at a big desk. She remembered who I was, Ma. And you too. 'It's you, Connor,' she said. 'And how's your mother?' I think she meant the bruise. She shook hands with Doreen and me.

"'They have come to work for you, Aunt Susan,' Bertha told her. You could tell she was proud to be showing us off. Miss Anthony wanted to know how old we were and where we went to school, things like that. She asked if St. Stephen's was a school for girls. We told her it was half-and-half, boys on one side with their own door and girls on the other. Next, she wanted to know what we were studying, and when we told her, she said she'd started just like us, learning to read and write and spell, the same as I'm doing for you, Ma. And do you know what her father did? He built a big new house when he moved to New York State where he set a schoolroom aside for Aunt Susan and her sisters. He hired a teacher from the women's seminary.

"They had poetry and exercises called cal—something, I can't say it. She would have gone on talking for a long time, but Bertha said we had to get to work and took us away. Miss Anthony liked to talk about how it was in the olden days, Bertha said, but right then she had to prepare her talk for the convention."

Connor finished supper and spread her arithmetic and reading books on the kitchen table. She wouldn't have time to work with her mother on her reading and sums for a while. When the excitement was over and she was coming straight home again they could take up the lessons. No more visits to Ten Broeck Street after that, she realized sadly. They hadn't done much today, but it had been fun to stand to one side and watch the bustle. "Do you reckon they know what they are doing?" Doreen had whispered, and they both giggled. Bertha had seen them and sent them around the house into all the rooms to gather the trash and take it to the basement.

"Before you start on your books, child, answer me a question," Connor heard Ma say. "And a truthful answer, mind you, no fairy stories."

Startled, Connor said, "I will, Ma. I always do. What is it?"

"They truly need me in the afternoon, like you say? I can't be of use like the other women, but I don't mind helping in the kitchen and with the wash or whatever wants doing, but I don't want to be in the way because your Bertha is feeling sorry for me."

"That's not it, Ma. I told you as soon as I came home what Bertha said. I asked because you and I talked about it and because I could see right away her aunt was having troubles. And about the money too. You wanted to be a volunteer, that's the word they use, just like the suffragists. I'll do what you do, Ma. That way we'll be together. Doreen can go do other things."

"You will do what Miss Hall and her aunt tell you, Connor O'Shea. That's for them to decide, not you. I was asking for myself. I had to get it straight before I went knocking at the door, me a grown woman, with you and Doreen Kruger beside me."

"I know, Ma. I'll come here to get you after school."

"I can find my way, thank you," her mother said. "I'll meet you at Northern Boulevard, is that agreed?"

Connor nodded and turned to her arithmetic. Sister had started them on long division, and the homework was hard. Doreen has her father to help her with the arithmetic, Connor thought jealously. She wondered how much arithmetic Da had studied in school before he'd dropped out. He brought home his pay on Saturdays and laid it on the table for Ma to look after. It was Ma who paid the bills and carried the accounts in her head. What was left each week she put aside in a leather purse in the ribbon drawer. When Da was of a mind to go to the saloon, he helped himself to the house money.

Connor wished the figures weren't so long. The addition and the multiplication she could do, but the long division slipped away from her when she got down to the carrying over. What had Miss Anthony been saying to them before Bertha took them away? Something like it was the arithmetic they would need when they grew up. "It's money that runs the country," she'd said, "and you'd better be able to understand it." Bertha had agreed. Connor copied the next problem and forced herself to pay attention.

Toward ten o'clock they heard Da's heavy steps. They were slow and stopped for a bit when he came to the landing at each floor. Connor looked at her mother. She closed the reader and made a place at the kitchen table. She seemed calm tonight, not anxious the way she was last week when Da started coming in late.

Her father pushed into the kitchen. He stood in the doorway breathing heavily. He had been drinking, you could tell right away, but he was steady on his feet. "I'll not be wanting my supper, Nora," he announced. "I ate with the boys."

That meant that he and some of his friends had gone to the saloon and had the pickled eggs and cheese and meat they put on the bar for the men who came in for beer and whiskey. Ma nodded and tidied the kitchen.

"No welcome do you have for me, wife?" Da asked. "No kind greeting for a man coming home from his day's work? Or from you, lass? Have you stopped altogether from coming to the capitol to visit with your da and telling him what the boys are up to along the Beaverkill?"

Her mother answered for them both. "You've not come straight home from work, Donal. You've come home from the Black Shamrock or some other place. You will tell me it was work and for all I know about it, maybe it was. But to me, it was drinking with Jocko Conlan and Malone and Shanahan and some of the others."

"And Tom Phelan, Nora my love, don't forget him. Senator Tom Phelan."

"It's Tom now, is it, Donal? You were making your plans, were you?"

"Aye, we were making our plans. This week and the one after, the senator says, we'll be ready for Miss Susan B. Anthony. We will have control of the sit—the sit-u-a-tion, that's what we will have."

Ma only nodded. "Off to bed now with you, Connor. Put your books in place. Your clean clothes for tomorrow are on the bed."

CHAPTER TWENTY-ONE

Miss Catherine came to the door almost as soon as Connor pulled the shiny brass bell knob. "Bertha is busy somewhere," she explained. "There is absolute confusion inside." And to Ma, "You're Connor's mother? I was hoping, praying, really, that you would come. We are having our problems today. Come in, please. Connor, Bertha said you and Doreen were to help sort the pamphlets and put them in envelopes. Your mother will be in the kitchen."

Two middle-aged women were standing at the huge table in the dining room taking booklets and pamphlets from open boxes. One of them, wearing her red-ribboned bonnet, smiled briefly at Connor and Doreen. "Bertha said we'd have help this afternoon. This material just arrived from the printer. I'm Clara Abbott and this is Sarah Carter. We've come up from New York City to do what we can."

"What are we to do?" Doreen asked.

"There are four different books here. Some go in these

91

envelopes, some in these, and all four go in these. Here is a list of what is what. If you can take charge of that, Sarah and I will start to address the envelopes. Do you have the list, Sarah?"

Sarah Carter, who *wasn't* wearing a suffragist bonnet, held up some sheets of paper. "Bertha gave me pens and ink too. We'll use this end of the table." For the first time she looked at Connor and Doreen. "I have two girls about your age, one eleven and the other almost fourteen, Felicity and Edwina. I could have brought them, I suppose. What do you think, Clara?"

"I doubt that Bertha has room for any more of us. How did you girls get involved?" she asked briskly.

Mrs. Abbott was staring at Connor's boots and heavy brown jumper. Connor felt her face turning red. Next to Doreen in her new cotton jumper and lace blouse, she felt like a scarecrow. "I was on the street next to the capitol building where Bertha was handing out pamphlets," she said quietly. She lifted a stack of booklets from a box. They were the pamphlets Bertha was offering people. "She was giving these away."

"Oh," Mrs. Abbott said. "Just like that, Bertha recruited you? It sounds like her."

Connor didn't know what to reply. It wasn't any of the woman's business how she came to be there. She hadn't asked Mrs. Abbott what she was doing in Albany. Ma would agree, she was sure, that it was none of Mrs. Abbott's business. Connor turned to Doreen. "Is that all of them?" she asked.

Doreen nodded. Of the four little books, one was the pamphlet they had already seen, another contained a list of men and women who supported woman suffrage, the third was a pamphlet titled *Woman Suffrage Now*, and the fourth, a little book with a blue cover, was titled *The Story of Susan B. Anthony*.

"Can we have one of these?" Doreen whispered.

"I don't know," Connor said. "We'll ask Bertha later. I want one, too."

The two women brought chairs to the table. Ignoring Connor and Doreen, they began addressing the envelopes that the girls stuffed and placed in front of them. They gossiped quietly about some of the other suffragists. Connor couldn't quite hear, but it sounded like they weren't saying anything very kind. She bent over her task and tried not to listen.

"Teatime," Bertha announced from the hallway. She placed a tray of tea and sweet biscuits beside Sarah Carter and Clara Abbott. "Connor, Doreen, you two come with me. I need your help."

In the kitchen Connor's mother and Bessie were preparing trays of tea and assorted cakes and cookies. Ma smiled at Connor. She lifted a pot from the back of the stove. "How many more, miss?" she asked Bertha Hall.

"Bertha, Mrs. O'Shea. Bertha, please. It will save us time if I am Bertha and you are . . . "

"Nora, miss."

"Good. You are Nora and I am Bertha. Connor and Doreen are to take these two trays to Miss Susan B. Anthony, where they will have *their* tea. You carry the pot and cups, Doreen. We'll entrust the sweets to Connor. You know where the library is, don't you?"

"Yes," Connor and Doreen answered together.

Connor knocked at the heavy carved door. "Come," a voice replied. "Here," Aunt Susan ordered, "on the low table. We'll have our tea here. My back is stiff from leaning over that desk. The chair is too low or the desk is too high, I can't decide which. What have you girls been doing?"

"Putting things in envelopes. There are two women addressing them, Sarah Carter and Clara something."

"Clara Abbott. From New York City. I think they came up the river to get out of the house for a while. But we can use them. New York is the most important state in the union. If we could carry the day here, half the battle for woman suffrage would be won."

"There's a book about you out there," Doreen went on. "It's not very big."

"Oh, that!" Aunt Susan smiled. "It's a little thing the suffragists put together. I can't imagine why they are passing that around. It makes me look like a dragon." Miss Anthony sipped her tea and nibbled on a chocolate cookie. "We'll have tea every afternoon while I'm here at Bertha's," she said. "Just the three of us. Is that agreeable?"

"Yes, ma'am," Connor said.

"I never get a chance to talk to young people," Aunt Susan went on. "Just grown-ups. I already know what they are going to say to me, and they know what I'm going to say to them. It's not very exciting. What time do you get out of school?"

"Three o'clock," Doreen replied.

"And you start at eight?"

"Yes, ma'am."

Miss Anthony was silent for a moment. She appeared to be thinking about something far away. "I was a teacher

94

when I was a young woman," she said. "For a while in a little town not far from Albany. I used to visit a teacher of mine here. I come back from time to time."

Miss Anthony paused again. She poured herself half a cup of tea and studied the pastries left on the plate. "Which ones do you girls like best?" she asked.

Connor pointed to a molasses square and Doreen to a vanilla tart. "Good," Miss Anthony said. "Then I'll have this one." She took the meringue that crunched as she bit into it. "I was thinking earlier about those days, and it occurred to me that I grew up mostly in the company of women—cousins, friends, teachers—and one man, my father. Some of us were so busy we never got around to marrying. So now I have no children or grandchildren to talk to me. That has been a loss, I believe. For a while now, I'll borrow you two."

Aunt Susan took a handkerchief from her sleeve, took off her glasses, and polished them with it. Her heavy dark satin dress crackled as she moved. When she had finished she set the glasses squarely on her nose. "I must have missed out on a great deal in my life. What do you girls think?"

This wasn't the way Sister Mary F. talked to them, Connor thought. She was going to grow old without a family, too. "I don't know," she replied cautiously. "Our teachers are all sisters, so they don't talk about such things."

"Well, I shouldn't do so, either," Miss Anthony said. "Back to your work. I'll take that last little cake. Tell Bertha thank you."

CHAPTER TWENTY-TWO

IT WAS AFTER SEVEN WHEN CONNOR AND HER MOTHER left the Hall mansion. Doreen had gone home an hour before in the carriage with her father. "Ma can't leave now," Connor told Mr. Kruger when he offered them a ride to Canal Street. "It's a nice evening and we'll walk, thank you. My father won't be home until late."

"Martha left this morning," her mother told Connor when they finally set out. "Bessie and I had to fix supper."

What had Ma prepared? Connor wondered. There hadn't been time to make potatoes and soda bread and roast a joint of meat. She didn't think the suffragists would enjoy the plain food Ma prepared for Da and her.

"There's a cold cellar," Ma explained. "I never before saw the likes of it. Bessie told me it stayed chilled the year around, even in the summer heat. Martha had laid in enough food for an army. All we had to do was bring up a joint of lamb and a piece of cold beef and carve it. With the squash and cabbage, we had the supper ready. I made some sandwiches for us to take home for our supper."

Connor remembered Martha fussing at Catherine the day before. "Why did she leave, Ma? Bertha and Aunt Catherine aren't like Mrs. Phelan. I wouldn't mind working for them."

"You aren't thinking of going into service, are you, lass? Martha left, according to Miss Catherine, because the work was more than she could do. Four more women came in last night on the train from Boston, and they had to make room for them up in the top of the house. Martha told Bessie her old legs wouldn't take it."

"What will they do?" Connor asked. "Doreen and I counted the people. There are twenty-four and maybe some we missed."

"I told Miss Catherine I could fill in until the convention, mornings too. Miss Catherine will let me do the Phelans' wash in the laundry. There's a drying room, too, Connor, and an ironing room with a little stove just for the irons. You never saw such a house. There's a room for everything. It's like the great Irish country houses where the English landlords set themselves up."

"Will you tell Da?" Connor asked.

"I think not," her mother said. "He would be after me that I hadn't asked him and what about the shirts he brought home from the assemblymen. If he were to find out we were working for the suffragists, you know he would be against it. It is best to leave some things unsaid."

Ma touched her cheek and winced. "Bessie said you could hardly see it. Right off she wanted to know if my old man gave me a whack. Her da is over sixty and still punches her mother on a Saturday night when he comes home drunk. Bessie couldn't put up with it when she grew up, she said, so she took the maid's job at Miss Hall's. Her ma says it's her husband's right, and she won't listen to Bessie. Like I used to put up with Donal when I didn't know any better. Well, here we are home, Connor. It makes a difference how close Canal Street is when you're talking and not counting the steps. We can eat the sandwiches while we do our homework."

Connor saved her spelling homework for last because it was the easiest. When she had finished, she placed it on top of her other books at the end of the kitchen table. She picked up the little blue book about Susan B. Anthony. "Look, Ma," she said. "Bertha said Doreen and I could each have one. It's what we put in some of the envelopes that we're going to take around tomorrow afternoon to the houses on Arbor Hill."

Her mother took the book to hold in two hands. She turned it over slowly, opened it to a page which she studied, closed the book and read the title, aloud, *The Story of Susan B. Anthony*. "A whole book about herself," she marveled. "Can you imagine, lass? Are you planning to write a whole book about your old ma someday, Connor?" she teased. "Read me a bit, Connor. My poor eyes are aching from that storybook you brought me. Some of those stories are a real task."

"I'll skim over it, Ma, some every night. It says here on the first page she grew up in a happy family where everyone was equal. It was in Massachusetts, out in the country, where her father had a cotton mill. When she was six they moved to New York State."

Connor paused to push ahead. There were two or three pages about Susan's father, which she scanned. Some of it she didn't understand. "I don't know some of the words, Ma. Mr. Anthony was a radical Quaker, it says. What do you suppose that means?"

To Connor's surprise, her mother answered right away. "We had a few Quakers in County Clare. Most of us were Catholic, but there were some others, too, Protestants and some Quakers who were different from the rest. It wasn't a proper faith, the Quakers said, no preachers or books or anything. Freethinkers they were, who wanted to do good for others, or so they said. Plain people they were, no parties or dancing for the Quakers."

"And 'radical,' what is that?"

"Ah, radicals, we had them by the dozen. Irish patriots against the English rule, radicals they were called. Some of them got themselves hanged fighting for Ireland. Don't tell me Mr. Anthony got himself hanged."

"Killed, you mean, Ma?"

"Until they were dead, indeed I do."

Connor skipped ahead. It looked as though Aunt Susan's father would be all right. But Mr. Anthony must have been a real radical. He was against jewelry and colored ribbons as well as slavery and drinking. "Aunt Susan became a Quaker when she was thirteen. About then her da's business failed and he fell into debt, so Susan had to take up teaching early on to help the family out. One of the men teachers wanted to marry her, but she said no. That was when she was twenty years old, I think. Let's see, when she was twenty-six they moved close to Rochester. Remember Bertha telling us about the parade in Rochester?"

Connor closed the book. "That was the first chapter. I think that's about all there is about growing up. The rest must be about her works. I'll ask her tomorrow when we join her for tea. Doreen says old people like to remember back to when they were young."

CHAPTER TWENTY-THREE

CONNOR'S MOTHER WAS AT THE DOOR ALMOST THE SEC-
ond Doreen pulled the bell knob of the Hall mansion. She
put her arm around Connor and directed her toward the
kitchen. "You come along, too," she said to Doreen, who
lagged behind. From under the pantry counter, she took a
package which she handed to Connor.

"For me?" Connor asked, surprised. "What is it?"

"Open it and you will see."

Bessie wiped her hands on her apron and came close to
watch. "She wouldn't tell me, either, Connor," she said. "It
must be something special."

Connor unwrapped the package. Underneath the soft
wrapping was a dress, neatly folded, with a brown shoe on
either side of the box. Connor held the dress high to let it
unfold and held it close to her. It was a beautiful red-and-
dark-green plaid with a white lace collar. She heard Doreen
murmur, "It's so pretty. I've never seen a dress so pretty."

101

"Oh, Ma," Connor gasped. "Did it come from Rubin's?" That was where Doreen bought the clothes her mother didn't make for her.

"Yes," her mother said. "The shoes too. They're French, the assistant told me. Miss Catherine asked me this morning to go downtown to bring pastries from the German bakery. I knew you and Doreen would be taking the envelopes around this afternoon, so I went by Canal Street and took some money. I don't want my girl out on the street talking to rich women in that old jumper and those clodhopper boots looking like she just got off the boat."

"But, Ma . . . " Connor protested. "The money is for the house someday."

"We can't be worrying about a house that may never be, lass. Slip into the pantry and let us see how you look."

The shoes had thin laces and small leather heels that clicked on the tile floor. Connor held her hair up from the back of her neck. Maybe there was a ribbon in one of the kitchen drawers. Bessie would know.

"You look like a proper princess," Bessie said. "I'll fetch Miss Catherine to find a ribbon."

"You have a beautiful daughter, Mrs. O'Shea," Catherine said as she tied a green satin ribbon into a bow. "There's not a woman in the house who wouldn't give a fortune to have hair like Connor's. Bertha will be proud to have these two girls delivering Aunt Susan's packets. Fetch Doreen a yellow ribbon from the sewing room, Bessie. They'll look like sisters."

"I brought your Sunday sweater," Connor's mother said. "There's a chill air coming up from the river."

Bertha had packed two shopping baskets with the

envelopes. "We'll start with the Ten Broeck addresses. The rest of the week, we'll branch out to the other streets. Here is the list I have prepared."

"What do we do?" Doreen asked. "Just give the envelope to the maid?"

"I'd rather you didn't unless you have to. Ask to see the mistress of the house, Mrs. whoever's name is on the envelope. If she comes to the door, hand her the envelope and say something like, 'We hope you will support Susan B. Anthony and woman suffrage in New York. It's very important.' If she wants to talk, say Aunt Susan—call her Miss Anthony, not Aunt Susan—'will address the convention next Monday at the capitol building and we hope she will be there to support the movement.' If the mistress doesn't come to the door, emphasize to the maid that the lady is to receive the envelope right away. Good luck. You should be back by teatime."

Connor had never knocked on anybody's door that she could remember, except Bertha's, and Senator Phelan's back door when she and Ma delivered the wash. "You do the first one," she told Doreen. "Then I'll do the next one and we'll go back and forth."

"This is the Ambrose place," Doreen said. "I think my father said they own the tanneries."

A maid in a starched white cap and an apron over a gray uniform opened the door. "May we speak to Mrs. Ambrose, please?" Doreen asked.

The maid looked down at their baskets. "What are you selling? We don't want salespeople at the front, my mistress says. They must go to the back."

"We have something important for your mistress,"

Doreen said bravely. She paused. "It's from Miss Bertha Hall," she added.

"From Miss Hall, is it?" the maid said. "I'll tell Mrs. Ambrose."

"I think we'd better keep saying Bertha sent us," Doreen told Connor. "Even if they don't know her directly, they are bound to know who she is."

Mrs. Ambrose, a small, fat woman, appeared in the doorway, frowning. "You girls have something for me?"

Doreen handed her a blue envelope. "It's about woman suffrage. Miss Susan B. Anthony is in town to talk to the convention next Monday about the vote for women," Doreen said nervously.

The frown turned into a smile. "I know she is in town. You may tell her for me that I will be at the capitol. And thank you for the material. I'll ask Mr. Ambrose to read it, too."

Connor wrote Yes after Mrs. Ambrose's name. "That's to tell Bertha she will be there," she told Doreen. "I'll do just what you did, it worked so well."

By five o'clock the baskets were empty. "I guess we did all right," Doreen said, looking at the list of names. "At least half the women we talked to said they believe in what Miss Anthony is doing."

"They might believe," Aunt Susan said when they reported on their trip along Ten Broeck Street. "And maybe some of them will show up on Monday. But I've discovered over the years that after they talk to their husbands, they are apt to change their minds. Sad to say, it's the men we have to educate."

"Why don't the men want women to have the vote?"

Connor asked. The reasons Da gave her didn't make much sense, she had decided. Ma knew more about the world than he did.

"I wish I knew, Connor," Aunt Susan said. "I hear what they say, and I used to try to argue with men, but I have discovered it is a waste of time. They don't listen. I have come to believe they are afraid. Now isn't that silly, to be afraid of your wives and your mothers and your daughters? I suppose they are afraid of losing what they think they own as men—money, whiskey, votes, power, only the Lord knows what else. When you listen to what most men say, it all comes down to their being afraid of losing something."

Aunt Susan sipped her tea. "It's been a struggle all my life. Sometimes I think I'm the wrong person for the job. If only my father had let me have a lovely plaid dress like yours, Connor, and a yellow hair ribbon like Doreen's, I might have grown up to be a wife and a mother and stayed at home instead of gallivanting across the country speaking against whiskey and slavery and violence and urging the vote for women. Pesky Susan, they call me. What do you think?"

"Is that what you wanted?" Connor dared ask. It seemed strange to her that Aunt Susan who wanted so much for women to be free should want these ordinary things for herself. This new dress, pretty as it is, isn't going to change my life, Connor told herself. She'd become a nun first.

"Once I grew up," Aunt Susan answered, "there was never any time to think about ball dresses and beads and ribbons and parties. There were the slaves to be freed, my father said, and men to be liberated from whiskey, and children to be protected and educated with an open mind, and

105

women to be made citizens. After a while I discovered that *I* was afraid, too, afraid to put on a pretty dress and afraid to act like a normal woman. Isn't that foolish? I had to keep on being a pesky Susan. That really is a lovely dress, Connor."

"I never had one before," Connor said. "Only a Sunday dress, and it's plain and dark. Doreen has lots, don't you, Doreen?"

"It's only because my mother sews," Doreen said. "I don't care much. The sisters say we shouldn't let our heads be turned by what we wear. The sisters wear only black"— Doreen paused—"and they can't support the vote for women. They don't have much to choose, I guess."

Aunt Susan smiled. "One thing at a time, Doreen, my father used to say. 'Don't put too much on your plate,' he said. 'You might not be able to eat it all.' We'll save the sisters afterward."

CHAPTER TWENTY-FOUR

"THIS IS THE LAST OF THEM FOR NOW," BERTHA SAID, handing Connor and Doreen a basket of envelopes Friday afternoon. "We'll see what happens on Monday, Aunt Susan says, to decide what we will do next week. A good number of women on Arbor Hill have pledged their support. Maybe we have a chance in New York State after all."

"Miss Anthony doesn't think so," Doreen spoke up. "Someday, but not this year."

"That's just Aunt Susan," Bertha said bravely. "She's not one to count her chickens before they are hatched. And don't you and Connor say a word to the women here about what you heard. It would be discouraging to them, they have worked so hard and long. Hurry along now. Aunt Susan wants to read part of her speech to you when you get back."

"Why does she want to do that?" Connor asked.

"You'll have to find out from her," Bertha replied. "Now, scoot along."

When they were outside, Doreen said, "What do you suppose they'll be doing next week? I'd like to work inside for a while. My parents keep asking me about the women here, who they are and where they come from. They tell me I should get to know them. They could be important to me someday."

Doreen's parents, Connor realized, were busy planning Doreen's life for her. First to Miss Pugh's fancy school for girls. Next to some college for women in Massachusetts called Smith, not far, Doreen's father told her, from where Miss Anthony grew up. After that, Doreen wasn't sure what she was supposed to do, maybe study to be a doctor or a lawyer. One thing for sure, she told Connor, she wasn't going to work in her father's butcher shop. She wasn't even supposed to talk about her father being a butcher.

Connor was silent as Doreen chattered on about her future. She had a funny feeling in her stomach that something bad was about to happen in her life. Da and Ma scarcely spoke to each other. Ma was polite and brushed Da's jacket as carefully as ever in the morning. When he told her he'd be coming home late and took money from the purse before he opened the door to leave, she nodded that she had heard and bent her head over the wash.

Da would stand in the door for a moment, uncertain, it seemed to Connor, whether he should say something else, explain to Ma what was going on at the capitol the way he used to or ask if she wanted him to bring home shirts. Or maybe even ask for the first time about the bruise on her cheek and say he was sorry. In the end he said nothing, grunting good-bye to Connor and thumping down the stairs. Nor did he ask Connor again if she would be walking along with him on her way to school.

The last envelope in the basket was delivered to an old woman who came directly to the door herself. Leaning on her cane in the doorway of a huge brick house almost as grand as the Hall mansion, she told Connor and Doreen she had been with Susan B. Anthony many years ago when she came to Albany to work for the vote. She would be with her again at the capitol building, cane and all, come Monday, she promised. "Tell Susan that Dolly Delahouse will be there. See if she remembers me, Dolly Delahouse," she pronounced her name slowly.

Miss Anthony was at the open window of the library when the girls took in the tea and cookies. The afternoon breeze was moving the lacy curtains. "I do believe spring has come at last," she said. "You can never tell in this part of the world. All I remember of spring in Massachusetts was the mud underfoot and the dark empty branches of the sugar maples. But, one magical day when you weren't paying attention, you got up and went to the window where the sun was shining and there were tiny leaves on the trees and grass was growing where the mud had been. I feel in my old bones that this is the day spring has come to Albany. It's an unpleasant town in the best of the seasons, I find. Was it nice outside? I wish I had gone with you. The walk would have done me a world of good. I've been cooped up here in Bertha Hall's palace since the night I arrived."

"It was warm," Connor said. "And tulips were out close to the houses. That's what happened—what you said about spring, I mean—where we used to live, in Martinville. The mud went away and the leaves came out on the trees and the children played. Other times it wasn't much."

"I know Martinville," Miss Anthony said. "They have torn it down, I hear. Have you passed out the last of our material?"

Connor nodded. "Dolly Delahouse was the last one on the list. She wanted me to ask if you remembered her from the time you first came here for suffrage."

"Dolly Delahouse, Dolly Delahouse," Miss Anthony murmured to herself. "Good Lord, it's been so long, but I do recall the name. Is she a little woman with light hair and what we used to call a turnip nose? Would that be her?"

"Maybe," Doreen answered. "She wasn't very big and she had gray hair and walked with a cane. Is that her?"

"Perhaps. I can't be sure. We are all gray now, and I have a cane in my room. There have been so many women I've known in so many cities and states. I wish I could remember them all. Fifty years of struggle, half a century, mind you, of speaking out for what I thought was right. I wish I could somehow thank all the women, and the men, too, who have helped me along the way."

CHAPTER TWENTY-FIVE

AUNT SUSAN STRAIGHTENED HER SHOULDERS AND arched her back against the stiffness. She was taller than Connor had realized, really tall and strong like Ma. The tiredness faded from her face as she smiled at Connor and Doreen. She fingered the red shawl across her shoulders. "Part of my speaking uniform," she laughed. "My black china silk dress with its blue stripes on the sleeves, my white flowered collar, and my old red shawl. It's the red shawl that tells people Pesky Susan has come to town. Once I wore a lovely white lace shawl and no one knew who I was."

"Is that why the women wear red ribbons in their bonnets?" Doreen asked. "To let people know who they are, suffragists, I mean?"

"Yes. Radical red, they call it."

"Are you a radical?" Connor asked, recalling what Ma

had said about the Irish radicals. "The book says your father was a radical."

Miss Anthony seated herself at the little table and passed the tea. She studied the plate of cookies. "Why, Catherine has found some ginger men. I'll take one of those. Mother used to make them for our birthdays. No fancy cakes, my father said." She bit the head off the ginger man. "They taste just the same. Am I a radical? you asked, Connor. I suppose I am. Not so radical, I reckon, as my father, but he was a man, of course, and could dare more. And he grew up in radical times, right after independence. More likely, I would call him a man of principle. How is the chocolate meringue, Doreen?"

"Good," Doreen mumbled, her mouth full.

"Anyone who wants to change the way things are," Aunt Susan went on, "is a radical to the people who want to keep things as they are. That's what I am going to say on Monday to the delegates. I'm afraid I'm not going to be very polite. After fifty years I am tired of begging for our natural political right. The vote is not a gift or a privilege for men to extend. It is our right and I will tell them so to their faces."

Miss Anthony set her glasses firmly on her nose. "They want me to quit bothering them, Senator Phelan and his powerful friends, but I won't quit, I will never quit," she announced firmly. "But it's young women like Bertha and you two who will have to carry on. Someday all the women in America will have suffrage if you keep at it. You may be certain of that."

"Bertha says maybe the delegates will vote for the women of New York this time," Doreen said.

"That is what we all must think and tell ourselves until

112

it is so. New York is only a step, although the biggest, on the road to Washington. It is the senators and the congressmen in the capital of our country who must be persuaded to act for universal suffrage. That is our final goal. Until that time women will not be free."

Aunt Susan turned to the desk. She shuffled some sheets of paper into an order that pleased her. She stared seriously at Connor and Doreen. "I haven't finished my talk, but this is how I begin. I ask you to listen and think about what I say. Remember that I am talking only to men on Monday. Women will be there, of course, but they are not the ones who will decide."

Susan B. Anthony cleared her throat. "I am saddened," she began, "to be addressing on this historic day a delegation of men only in the capitol building of the great state of New York. Where are your wives, I ask you, where are your mothers and daughters? Where are the women whose mothers and grandmothers worked side by side with their men for a hundred years and more to build this state? I hope their spirit is here, because I speak for them."

Miss Anthony paused again to clear her throat. "You must ask yourselves today why men are sitting here alone to vote on this issue. Where are the women to whom suffrage means so much? Ask yourselves, if you are truthful, what is a democracy that denies half the people of this noble state their political liberty and equality."

Aunt Susan paused again to shift some sheets of paper. She went on, "It is no democracy, I say to you, which has freed the slaves and kept its women captives. It is no democracy which gives the vote to saloon keepers and drunkards and denies it to its women.

"How does that sound?" Aunt Susan asked the girls.

Connor looked to Doreen to reply. She sensed that Doreen might understand these things better than she did.

"Yes," Doreen said in a strong voice. "That's right. It's what Sister Mary Francis tells us, isn't it, Connor? It's what my father says, sort of. He says women are as good as men, but they aren't ready for the vote yet."

Aunt Susan shuffled through her papers once more. "Here it is," she explained. "I speak to that point. 'You will say that women are not ready for the vote. For forty years I have heard the cry go out, "Women are not ready to have the vote." If you ask men when their women will be ready, they reply they do not know, someday, to be sure, but not right now. Today I am here to tell you that the someday is today. Women *were* ready and women *are* ready. It is not tomorrow or the day after tomorrow. It is today.' Will you tell your father that, Doreen?"

"I don't know. I'll tell my mother first."

Aunt Susan put the papers on the desk. "There is more, but I won't keep you. Bertha probably needs you. Remember, Doreen, you, too, Connor, that you and your friends are the ones who will have to keep up the struggle. It will be a long march to Washington and equality."

Susan B. Anthony picked up the last ginger man. She broke it in two and gave Connor and Doreen each a half.

CHAPTER TWENTY-SIX

Doreen was already in the kitchen talking to Aunt Catherine when Connor and her mother arrived on Saturday morning.

"I have made a pot of hot chocolate," Catherine said. "Mrs. Kruger sent us a bag of fresh doughnuts that are delicious."

"My father brought me in the buggy," Doreen explained. "We would have come for you, but we didn't know what time. Miss Catherine says we are to help in the house today."

"Miss Anthony has the women who aren't downtown on the street corners writing letters to her friends here in Albany," Catherine explained. "A last request for help and encouragement, I believe. As soon as Bessie is organized we'll set the house straight. Tomorrow will be a busy day."

"Oh, good Lord," Connor's mother suddenly exclaimed. She put her hand over her mouth. "I'm sorry, miss. I just remembered the Phelans' wash downstairs. I finished it yesterday afternoon and we forgot to deliver it on our way home. There was the tea and the getting ready for the supper meal and . . . "

"You had every reason to forget, Mrs. O'Shea. I'm sure if you and Connor take it around to the senator's home now, it will be all right."

"I'll bring the basket up, Ma," Connor said. She stuffed half a doughnut in her mouth and headed for the laundry room. Ma had never been late before, and sometimes she was a day early if Mrs. Phelan wanted the wash on Thursday. Today—or yesterday—was payday too. She hoped Mrs. Phelan wouldn't be cross.

Agnes, the maid who took the laundry and brought Connor the hard candy, came to the back door. She said, "I'll get the mistress for you." She returned with Mrs. Phelan, who told her to take the basket upstairs.

Mrs. Phelan looked down at Connor and her mother from the top of the stoop. "I believe Friday is the day you are meant to deliver the laundry, Mrs. O'Shea, not Saturday morning, which is a great inconvenience to the servants and to me. I'm sure you must have a good excuse."

Connor's mother shook her head. "I forgot, ma'am. I was doing something else and I plain forgot."

"Something more important than your obligation to us, Mrs. O'Shea?"

Ma didn't answer right away. Connor saw her bite her lower lip, the way she did when she was angry with Da. "Yes, ma'am," she replied. "I believe it was more important, as you say."

116

"Then you must continue doing what is so important to you, Mrs. O'Shea, and we shall make other arrangements here." Mrs. Phelan went into the house, closing the door behind her.

"The money, Ma, the money," Connor blurted out. "Yesterday was the last Friday in April. She owes us."

Ma put her arm around Connor. "I won't disgrace myself by arguing like a fishwife with a fine lady. Never you care, lass. We won't let Mrs. Phelan make beggars of us. Let's hurry back. We have better things to do than whining about lost wages."

"But the house, Ma. It was the house money."

Her mother shook her head. "Your father is not of a mind these days to be planning for a house. He has taken the last of the money from the purse to buy whiskey for Senator Phelan and his friends," she said sadly. "He has become an important man."

"But when he is captain . . . " Connor argued.

"We will talk about it then, won't we, girl?"

At the end of the day, Bertha accompanied Connor and her mother to the door. "I cannot find the words to express our gratitude, Nora. I heard Miss Anthony already thanked you for all of us, and I could tell that she was moved. It is true she expects a great deal from her friends, but you were a stranger who wanted to help. She was deeply touched."

"She is a noble woman, Susan B. Anthony. She'll stay at what she is doing until she drops, so we must help her along the way, must we not, Connor? We will be here tomorrow after church, unless my husband is home. He is busy with Senator Phelan working against us."

"Connor told me something like that," Bertha said.

117

"You must not allow us to make your family life difficult, Nora."

Connor's mother smiled. "We will see, Miss Bertha."

"Bertha, Mrs. O'Shea, my name is Bertha."

Ma nodded and took Connor's hand. "It's getting dark, child. Let's hurry along."

Da was sitting at the table in his grey undershirt. He had turned up the coal-oil lamp, and his giant shadow spread across the wall in back of him. He had pulled off his boots and rested his stockinged feet on the table. His jacket lay on the floor next to an empty beer pail. He held a heavy glass in his hand. At the other end of the table he had dropped a bundle of shirts.

"Having yourselves a walk, were you? The spring air feels good these days." Da smiled. "What do you say we go down to the river after Mass tomorrow for a sausage and beer and watch the excursion boats? Like we used to, Nora?"

Da leaned back in his chair. "There's another pail of beer on the porch keeping cool. Fetch it for your old da, lass."

As Connor moved toward the door, her mother pushed ahead of her. She leaned out to take the beer, which she put on the table in front of Da.

"Have a glass with me, Nora, love, and a small one for the girl. It's an evening for celebration. I could be at the Shamrock with the boys, but Tom said it was proper for us to be with our families. We have been neglecting them, he said, making our plans for the crazy women. But now it's done, and we can all rest easy. The women will not have their way."

"What are you celebrating?" Connor's mother asked.

"I told you, Nora. The crazy women and their crazy Aunt Susan. We have a surprise ready for them come Monday morning. Tommy and some of the assemblymen and Tom's friends up from the city and me—me, too, Nora—have had our heads together. They won't make fools of us this time."

"It was you that played the fool last time, you said, Donal. Was it your friends as well?"

Da's smile disappeared. "That was then and now is now. We'll show them a trick or two. Fetch a glass and sit with me at the table. I had my supper at the Shamrock, so you'll not be needing to feed me. Sit you both down."

Connor and her mother took their places at the table. "We won't be drinking with you, Donal, but we'll listen to your tale of triumph over the women. What is your surprise?"

Da smiled again. He put the glass to his lips and emptied it. "It's a secret. We are all sworn to secrecy, but that crazy old woman will learn on Monday that she won't have her way with us a second time."

Connor's father pointed to the dirty shirts. "I brought you some shirts. The men want them back on Monday. Tommy said his wife told him you didn't deliver the wash yesterday. Mrs. Phelan was upset."

"She was," Ma said. "So upset she dismissed us on the spot this morning, did she not, Connor? And I won't be doing those shirts, either, Donal, you can tell your friends."

Da sat up straight in his chair. "That's not for you to say, woman. You can do the shirts before we go to the river tomorrow and iron them in the evening when we come back. I'll ask the senator to give you your job back with his missus. He'll see to it. Like Tommy says, we men have to stick together."

"What are you so afraid of, that you have to stick together?" Connor's mother asked.

"What do you mean, woman, 'afraid'?"

Without thinking, Connor spoke up. "That's what Miss Anthony told us, Doreen and me. She said men were against the vote for women, their wives and daughters and mothers, all of them, because they were afraid."

Da lurched to his feet, knocking over the pail of beer. His brow knit in a scowl of confusion. "What does she say, Nora?" he stammered. "Has the child lost her wits altogether? Talking to Susan B. Anthony? The child is daft."

"It's the truth, Donal. Sit down and listen to me. Your daughter and her friend Doreen Kruger take their tea with Miss Anthony. You should be proud of her. And I," Ma added proudly, "work with suffragists on Arbor Hill in the biggest house in Albany. They need me there, and your daughter as well. When the vote is taken I will return to my wash, the same as you will go back to your regular duties at the capitol."

Connor's father swung his fist. He caught his wife full on the cheek, knocking her into the corner. He stepped forward, fist drawn back to strike her again.

"No! No! Stop!" Connor screamed.

Her father turned. He seized Connor around the waist with one hand. With the other he loosed his leather belt. Shoving his daughter across the table, he struck her with the doubled belt, again and again and again.

CHAPTER TWENTY-SEVEN

CONNOR'S FATHER TOOK HIS HAND FROM HER NECK. HE stepped away, rocking on his stockinged feet and breathing heavily. Through her sobs, Connor heard his rough words. "I'm sorry, girl, but I promised you. I told you to **stay away** from those crazy women. You know I told you." He took a cloth from the shelf and with clumsy hands wiped at the beer on the table around Connor's body.

Connor didn't move. Face buried in her arms, trembling, she waited. She heard Da's curses as he threw the cloth to the floor, then heavy steps to the bedroom and the slamming of the door.

Connor hurried to the corner where Ma lay crumpled on her side, moaning. "Ma," Connor cried in her mother's ear. "Ma, can you hear me? He's gone to bed now. He's not here. Sit up, Ma." Connor took her mother's arm and helped her lean against the wall. Ma's eye was swelling. It was almost shut. Blood trickled from a cut on her cheek.

"You wait here," Connor told her. At the sink she dipped a cloth in the drinking bucket. She squeezed it tight and pressed it to her mother's face. Ma winced and shuddered. "Easy, lass, easy." She took the cloth from Connor and lightly wiped her cheek. "Now help me to my feet. My head is spinning."

Slowly, Connor's arm around her waist, Ma rose to her feet. Connor drew a chair from the table. "Sit here, Ma. I'll tidy up." She picked up the dirty rag from the floor.

"Leave it," her mother ordered. "It's Donal's doing and his to clean up. The carpetbag I brought from the old country, fetch it for me, child. You know where it is."

The heavy bag was tucked in a corner of the parlor behind the sofa. Connor crept past the bedroom door. In the dark she reached over the sofa. The old bag was awkward to lift. It carried smells Connor did not recognize. She sat for a moment on the sofa to catch her breath. They were leaving, that was what they were doing, she was certain. Ma had been changing from the time when Da took to drink again. Now she wasn't going to fight him anymore, and she wasn't going to nag. Connor remembered what Bessie had told Ma about her own mother. Ma wasn't going to be like Bessie's ma.

Her mother had wiped the kitchen table. "Put it here, lass. It still smells of smoke from the old cottage. Never mind, it will serve us. Go into your room and put on your Sunday dress and your new shoes. Leave the dress you're wearing behind. I don't want the smell of your da's beer with us. And those cloddy school boots, too, leave them under the bed. They were never meant for a girl's feet. Put your dress from Rubin's on top where it won't get wrinkled. And wear your sweater."

"Where are we going, Ma? To Kevin and Peg's place?"

Her mother put her finger to her lips. "Shh. First the doing, then the talking." She slipped out of her sleeves and tiptoed into the bedroom. She returned with an armful of clothes, which she tucked into the bag. "Turn your back," she told Connor. "I'm going to change into my Sunday dress. There's blood on my work dress. We'll leave it behind."

Ma buckled the bag and put her heavy coat around her shoulders. "Let us be off. Take a good look if you like. We'll not be coming back."

A damp fog floated up from the Hudson. Canal Street was empty. From downtown Connor heard drunken men shouting outside the saloons. They would go on until dawn. "Where are we going, Ma?" she asked again.

"We'll wait in Washington Park until the first Mass," her mother replied.

"But Kevin and Peg will take us in," Connor protested.

"And what will your da's cousin do when we go knocking on his door in the middle of the night?"

"Peg will make room," Connor explained.

"And while Peg is making room for us your Uncle Kevin will be slipping out the door to talk with Donal, and the two men will decide we two women ought to be with Donal and they will drag us back to the tenement, that is what will happen. I brought my wash money, Connor. We'll find ourselves a room tomorrow. I have the old blanket from your bed to put around us on the bench."

The iron bench in the park was cold and wet. Ma wiped the seat with a sheet of newspaper from the trash bin. "Put your head in my lap, Connor, and cover yourself."

"But we can share," Connor said.

"I have my coat. I can sit here and sleep. Many's the time I've done so in the kitchen when I took a rest from the irons."

Suddenly Connor felt weary. She lay on the bench, her head in Ma's lap, and closed her eyes. Ma smoothed her brow and hummed a familiar song from the old country. Before Connor could collect her thoughts, she was asleep.

When she woke up, the morning sun had burned off the evening fog. Connor looked up. Her mother was sound asleep, her head back, mouth half open. A funny noise gurgled deep in her throat.

"Ma," Connor said softly. "Wake up, you're going to choke."

Her mother's head snapped forward. She coughed and pulled the coat around her. "I was dreaming I was back in my village. It must have been the sight of the carpetbag that set me off. Old Mr. Curley was coming to court me, the one I told you about. Only he was older in my dream, bent over and wrinkled, and he wanted me for his wife. You woke me just in time. I might have said yes, mightn't I, and I wouldn't be here now in Washington Park with my girl. What time do you say it is, child?"

The sun was about where it was in the sky when she and Da went off in the morning. "It must be getting toward eight," Connor said.

"We've had a good sleep, then. We have already missed the first Mass. Stretch your legs and we'll be off to St.

Stephen's. I must look a horror, like an old village crone with one eye bunged shut."

"You look fine, Ma. It will go away like the other time. Anyway, Sister says God doesn't care how you look when you come to His house."

Ma laughed. She sounded almost happy. "Maybe not, but it's not God we'll be sitting next to in the pews. No matter, what is done is done. Sister is right, like always. He won't care." Ma lifted the carpetbag. "Off we go, child."

CHAPTER TWENTY-EIGHT

"WE'LL FIND OURSELVES A BOARDINGHOUSE THIS EVEN-ing," Ma said. "Bessie and I have a lot to do before tomor-row. The ladies will be wanting their dresses pressed and their undergarments starched and ironed. You put yourself in charge of their shoes and boots. Will Doreen be here today?"

"I don't think so," Connor said, pulling the bell knob. "Give me the bag, Ma. Maybe Bessie won't ask questions if I am carrying it." She took the carpetbag from her mother's hand as Bessie opened the door and stood to one side to let them pass.

"It's a madhouse already," Bessie confided. "You'd think most of these women never had to lift a finger to do for themselves." She stared at Connor's mother for a minute. "You sit here, Mrs. O'Shea, and Connor will give you a cup of tea from the stove. I'll be straight back."

Bessie returned with a brown jar. With the top off, it

smelled of camphor. "Lift up your face," she ordered. She rubbed the pungent white salve into the bruised skin and around the swollen eye. She stood back. "That's better, isn't it, Connor? It's what I used to do for my own ma. Now you sit and rest today, Mrs. O'Shea, when it gets too much for you. Connor and I will make do. Your girl will be ready for going into service someday, Mrs. O'Shea. It's better," she whispered into Connor's ear, "than being a nun or marrying some brute of a man. I'll fetch Miss Catherine and we'll lay out our work for the day."

Connor cut two slices of raisin cake at the breadboard. She buttered them and put the plate next to her mother. She poured herself a cup of tea. "It looks fine, Ma. Does it hurt much?"

Her mother shook her head. "The camphor makes it cool," she said. "It's the eye that troubles me. It's as tight as a drum. And my head feels uneasy."

"Remember when Keefe fell down at the Beaverkill and struck his head?" Connor asked. "His eye was closed for a week, but there was no harm done. We'll keep a cool cloth on it."

Bertha marched into the kitchen, followed by Aunt Catherine and Bessie. She took Connor's mother by the arm. "Come with us, Nora," she ordered. "Bessie, bring the bag up. You come, too, Connor. You can help."

Bertha led Ma up the steps. She turned to the right at the head of the stairs. At the end of the hallway she pushed open the door to a large bedroom. It contained two beds, a small sofa, a large bureau, and a heavy wardrobe. "Rest on the sofa, Nora, while Bessie changes the linen."

"But, miss . . ."

"Bertha."

"I can't be staying here, Bertha. The room is for Miss Anthony's people."

"Clara and Sarah left early this morning for New York. They said they had to get back to their families, but Aunt Susan said their hearts weren't in the suffrage movement. Sometimes I think Aunt Susan doesn't understand the sacrifices women have to make. No matter, you and Connor are to stay here. Later we can talk. Catherine will get you settled in."

Should she tell Bertha what had happened? Connor wondered. It looked as though Bessie might already have said something. She'd best remain quiet. She gathered the sheets and pillow slips Bessie had taken from the beds. "I'll put these in the laundry room," she said.

Downstairs Miss Catherine told Connor that she would be in charge of the kitchen. "The others and I will help out, Connor, but you will be the one in charge. Bessie and I are needed upstairs today. Can you do it? You know where everything is now, don't you?"

"Yes, ma'am. I'll put a cold luncheon on the buffet. I'm not sure about supper—I guess you call it dinner. I can only cook potatoes and cabbage and boil a piece of ham."

"Then we'll have potatoes and cabbage for supper, won't we?"

Connor laid out the plates and silverware on the sideboard. A pitcher of water, a pitcher of milk, and, later, two pots of tea, Catherine had said. Then Connor went down to the cold room. On Thursday Ma had cooked a turkey and a loin of pork. There was enough left for lunch, she decided. Cold beets and pickled peaches perhaps; there were dozens of jars of each on the shelves. She'd cook the potatoes and cabbage for supper. That ought to take care of everything for today. By noon the sideboard was ready.

"You are a magician," Catherine exclaimed. "I'll finish here. Miss Anthony is with your mother. Why don't you go up?"

Aunt Susan was seated on the sofa talking to Ma, who was propped up in bed with two pillows at her back. Connor sat on the edge of the bed that would be hers.

Aunt Susan nodded to Connor. "And what do you plan for the future, Mrs. O'Shea?" she asked.

"The girl and I will take a room. We have a little money. I can find employment or I can go into service, if they have room for Connor."

"And when your husband orders you to return?"

"No," Ma said. "Not now or ever. We are quits, Donal and I."

"He may keep after you, Mrs. O'Shea. The law will be on his side, I am sorry to tell you. He may say you have stolen the girl. And your priest, he will surely urge you to return to your husband. It will be your duty, he will say."

"No," Ma said again. "I will take my daughter and leave. We will go downriver to the city. Donal will not follow us there. He will stay here with his friends at the Black Shamrock. That is all Donal wants, anyway, to drink and have someone tell him what to do."

"Perhaps you are right. You must be strong, Mrs. O'Shea. You will be alone and unprotected, and the world will try to have its way with you."

"Connor and I can face the world. We will be as hard as we have to be."

"I believe you will be," Miss Anthony said. "You appear to be an extraordinary woman. You are a fortunate child, Connor. You don't want to bring charges against your husband, Mrs. O'Shea?"

"He's an officer of the law, Miss Anthony. What good will that do? Let him go his way, we will go ours."

"Did you tell her what Da said about tomorrow, Ma?" Connor asked, realizing that Miss Anthony had better be told about the surprises Senator Phelan had prepared.

Her mother shook her head. "You tell her, child. You understand it better than I."

"My father told us that Senator Phelan and his friends have planned a big surprise for you tomorrow. He wouldn't tell us what."

"I would be surprised if they hadn't," Aunt Susan said calmly. "I have dealt with Tommy Phelan and his friends before, here and in New York City. I will warn Bertha. I should think they will try to close the doors of the capitol to keep out the women who want to hear what the speakers have to say. They have done that in other states."

Aunt Susan arose and stretched her back. "The spirit is willing"—she laughed—"but the flesh is failing. We will talk later, after tomorrow's excitement."

"I'll bring you a plate, Ma. I prepared the lunch all by myself, every bit of it. Miss Catherine said it was a miracle."

"Bring two plates, lass. We'll have our meal in our room like the fancy folks."

CHAPTER TWENTY-NINE

"AT RECESS," SISTER MARY FRANCIS TOLD THE CLASS, "we will walk down to the capitol. This is a historic day, and you will be able to witness it. When your children read about it someday, you can tell them you were there."

"What's happening at the capitol?" Patricia Walsh asked.

"A famous woman named Susan B. Anthony is going to speak about the right of women to vote. I will try to persuade them to let you in. We can stand at the back of the chamber."

"Will we miss recess?" Patricia asked.

"Yes, and perhaps part of your lunchtime too."

Most of the girls groaned. Sister Mary Francis slapped her ruler hard on the desk. "I am ashamed of you. I don't want to hear another word. We will march like young ladies, two by two, on the pavement. You will hold hands until we come to the capitol. You will not laugh or giggle or push or talk loudly. I'll be watching every one of you."

"What if Da sees me?" Connor whispered to Doreen. She realized as soon as she spoke that Da couldn't get at her anymore. She could listen to Susan B. Anthony make her speech and her father couldn't do a thing about it.

"What's the matter?" Doreen replied. She had not heard.

"Nothing," Connor said. "I was wondering if we would see my father."

As the class walked down the street, they heard angry voices. Sister Mary Francis marched to the head of the line. She held up her hand signaling the girls to stop. The voices grew louder and angrier.

"Let us go slowly," Sister Mary Francis called. "And stay close together. If there is trouble on the streets, we will return to the school at once. Connor, you and Doreen skip ahead to see what is going on. Be careful and don't go near."

From the corner where Bertha had handed out her pamphlets, they could see a crowd of women in their red-ribboned bonnets. They were pressing against the doors of the building, which were guarded by the capitol police. Connor thought she saw Da in the middle pushing the women back, but in the confusion she couldn't be certain. The women were demanding entry. Some of them were shaking their fists at the police.

Well-dressed men pushed their way through the gathering. Each held out a slip of paper to the guards and scooted inside when the door was cracked open. Connor heard cries of, "No, No."

The number of women increased. They were becoming angrier. "We'd better report back," Connor told Doreen. "I don't think Sister wants us to get any closer."

"You were right, Connor," Sister Mary Francis said on their return. "We will wait right here where we can retreat in a hurry if we have to. Perhaps they are letting the delegates in first. There may not be enough room for the women."

"I don't think so," Connor said. This was Da's secret plan. They weren't going to let the women in where they could influence the delegates. They must have given passes to the delegates, she decided.

"I want to go back to St. Stephen's," Patricia wailed.

"Stand closer together," Sister Mary Francis ordered. "We are perfectly safe. This is part of history, too. You, Patricia, stop howling. Connor and Doreen will be our scouts. Maybe we will see Miss Anthony when the fuss is over. Go up to the corner, you two, and keep us informed."

The noise from the crowd died away. A single loud voice took its place. It sounded familiar.

"Hurry!" Doreen said to Connor. "It sounds like Bertha."

The women had turned away from the doors to listen to Bertha who stood on the steps calling for their attention. "Stand together," she commanded. "All the way across the steps. Stand firm, arm in arm. Do not budge. If we cannot go in, we will not allow anyone else in. Stand firm. Do not let anyone push through."

The women formed solid lines across the steps. As the delegates in their suits and bowler hats approached, Bertha asked them to stand back. Uncertain, the men withdrew.

"I'll report to Sister," Connor said. "You stay here." Excitedly Connor reported to Sister Mary Francis that the women had formed barriers against the men who wanted to enter. "I think the class can come up to the corner now," she said.

As the girls approached the crossing, the noise of bells ringing and horses clopping on the cobbles sounded up from State Street. A line of heavy black carriages, one policeman driving, another beside him pulling on the bell cord, and a third officer swaying on the back step, rolled to the capitol steps. When the carriages had passed Connor and Doreen raced across State Street to join the class.

"The Black Marias," Connor said. Da had told her about these city police wagons. "I've been inside one or two in my time, on a Saturday night," he'd told her. "On a Saturday night when the boys and I drank a glass too much and made a public nuisance of ourselves outside the Shamrock. The city police would shove us into the wagons and take us to the station until we quieted down and were able to walk home by ourselves."

Now the officers in the back of the carriages opened the doors. Inside, Connor could see two rows of benches. The other officers marched up to the lines of women. "Clear the steps, ladies," the captain said. "You are committing a public nuisance and I ask you to desist. Clear the steps, ladies, and let the gentlemen pass through."

"Do not move," Bertha cried. "We are citizens. We have a right to be here. Stay where you are."

The captain and one of his men moved to either side of Bertha and led her to the first Black Maria. Bertha crossed her wrists in front of her like the woman handcuffed on the front of the pamphlet.

One by one, without protest, the women in red-ribboned bonnets followed Bertha Hall to the wagons. When the

134

first was filled, the officer latched the doors and knocked on one side with his stick. The driver cracked his whip over the two black horses. The second officer clanged the bell while the carriage rolled onto State Street and down the hill. The driver tipped his hat politely to Sister Mary Francis.

Among the last of the women carried away was Dolly Delahouse. Limping along on her cane, head high, Miss Delahouse spurned the officer's helping hand, and climbed painfully into the wagon. "For shame," Sister Mary Francis shouted at the policeman.

"For shame," she repeated, louder this time. "Back to the school, class; we have seen enough of this disgrace."

"What about Miss Anthony and the other speakers for the vote?" Doreen asked.

"They will be inside the capitol building," Sister Mary Francis told her, "making their speeches to the deaf ears of ignorant men. It is a sad day for democracy, girls, a sad, sad day. Don't you be forgetting it."

CHAPTER THIRTY

"WELL, NOW, YOU WERE THERE, OUTSIDE THE STATE house, the two of you, and you saw what went on?" Susan B. Anthony asked.

"Yes. Sister took us to the capitol to hear you talking to the delegates," Doreen answered. "We didn't see you, and Sister said you were bound to be inside giving your speech. Was it what you read to us?"

"Just about. I called Senator Phelan and his minions some unpleasant names before I started in. He was smiling like the cat that swallowed the canary, as well he might. He and his people have the power, and the delegates are eating out of his hand. They sat there quiet as mice listening to my friends and me telling them how they *ought* to behave. Then they let us leave, so they could have their discussions."

"How come they didn't arrest the women?" Connor asked. By the time school let out and she and Doreen reached Ten Broeck Street, Bertha and the suffragists were hard at work inside. They had been taken to the police station, Bertha told them, and given a lecture by a magistrate and turned out into the streets.

"They were arrested, Connor," Miss Anthony explained, "but not charged. The senator had it all planned. He anticipated that the suffragists would bar the door, and he had the police wagons waiting down the street. I expected that to happen, so Bertha and I planned to make the best of it. The sight of respectable women arrested on the steps of the capitol building of the great state of New York will set a number of men and women thinking. At least, we hope it will. Senator Phelan will pay a price for what he did. I hope it will keep him out of the governor's mansion someday."

"What about the vote? Will the delegates vote for suffrage when they find out what happened outside?" Connor asked.

"Maybe a few of them will feel bad enough to give us their support. That's what Bertha thinks."

"What about you? What do you think?" Doreen asked.

"I am older than Bertha by half a hundred years. I have seen these things happen before. As I told you, it's a long road to Washington. Sometimes it's one step forward and two steps backward, sometimes it's the other way around. Now let's see what we have for tea today. Why, it's currant bread and butter."

"My mother made that," Connor said proudly. "She didn't have time to go to the bakery."

"It is delicious," Aunt Susan said. "Your mother is feeling better today."

"Yes, ma'am. She'll be all right now."

"Is your mother sick, Connor?" Doreen asked.

Connor felt uncomfortable. Doreen was her best and only friend, but she did like to gossip. Connor didn't want what happened Saturday night to get all around St. Stephen's. She saw Aunt Susan looking at her. She smiled the little smile she had and nodded her little nod the way she did when she wanted you to do something or approved of something you had just done or said. It meant she should tell Doreen.

"We're living here now, Ma and I," Connor said. "Upstairs at the end of the hall. Da got real drunk Saturday night and was mean to Ma and me, and my mother decided it was enough, so we packed up and left."

It came out easier than she had feared. "Guess where we spent the night, Doreen? On one of those benches in Washington Park. It was, oh, so damp and cold, but Ma put a blanket over me and I fell asleep right away. We slept so hard we missed the first Mass. Then Bertha gave us a room."

Doreen was impressed. "You can stay with us, I'll bet. We have an extra room. I'll ask my parents."

"Why don't you wait awhile, Doreen?" Aunt Susan said. "Let things begin to work themselves out. Tell me, Connor, your father is a capitol policeman?"

"He's the sergeant," Connor answered, somewhat proudly. "He works with Senator Phelan."

"A tall man with a nice smile under his mustache?"

"Sometimes, when he's not cross. Did you see him?"

"Indeed I did. It was your father who escorted me into the assembly room as though I were Queen Victoria, all smiles and gentle courtesy. He made me feel for a moment that I was someone important. Afterward, he went straight outside to bar the door, Bertha said."

Connor nodded. "I saw him. He wouldn't let any of the women in, except the women speakers."

"But he had such a fine smile. That's something, I suppose," Miss Anthony remarked. "Now I have to get back to work. We have exactly one week to make the most of this."

"What are you going to do?" Doreen wanted to know. "Will you write another speech?"

"It is not the time for more speeches. Everyone knows what I have to say. The Lord knows I've said it often enough. The delegates will discuss and argue and make their deals, and next Monday morning they will decide for us or against us. In either case I will take the train to California and start in there. In the meantime we will all sit down and write letters. We want every suffrage supporter from New York City to Rochester in front of the capitol next Monday morning when the delegates assemble. We want those men to have a good look at the women who support the vote."

"You're going to live here with Bertha?" Doreen whispered when they had closed the library door. "Wait until I tell Pa."

"Only for a week, I think," Connor said. "They need Ma here all the time until the women go home. Then Miss Catherine and Bessie can look after the house for Bertha until they find someone to take Martha's place. Ma says we'll find a room and she'll get a job or go into service. After I finish school next year, I'll have a job too."

"You're not going back to Canal Street ever?"

139

"No, not ever. Da's not going to stop drinking, Ma says. And she's made up her mind she's not going to do laundry for the rest of her life, either. 'We'll have ourselves an adventure,' she told me. 'You and me, lass, it's us against the world.' That's what she said. Anyway, come down to the laundry room. We have to start working. Bessie and Ma changed the linens on all the beds today, and Ma is doing the wash."

"But I don't know how," Doreen protested.

"It's easy," Connor said. "I'll teach you how to use the irons. You can start on pillow slips. They're the easiest of all."

"All right," Doreen agreed, "but you have to promise me one thing."

"What's that?"

"You don't ever tell my pa," Doreen said.

CHAPTER THIRTY-ONE

TUESDAY MORNING SISTER MARY M. STOOD IN FRONT OF the classroom scowling at the late arrivals and slapping a ruler in the palm of her hand. She fixed Connor and Doreen with a threatening look as they pushed into their desks. "Heads down," she ordered, and raced through the morning prayer.

Next, the sister studied a sheet of paper. "You have arithmetic now, it says here. Long division." Her glance shifted from girl to girl until it lingered on Connor. "You, Connor O'Shea, divide eight hundred ninety-nine by sixty-seven."

"Yes, Sister," Connor whispered. She reached for her workbook.

"In your head, Connor O'Shea. Do the division in your head. Anyone can do it on a piece of paper."

"I'll try, Sister." Connor began writing the figures in her hand with her index finger. "Let's see, that's sixty-seven into eighty-nine. That's one time and you take away, wait a minute, you take away a two, and another two. Twenty-two. Then . . . "

"We don't have all day to find out," Sister Mary M. snapped. "Connor, you may stay after school to finish."

"But, Sister . . . " Connor began.

Sister Mary M. hit the desk with her ruler. She went around the room. Half the class could not answer her questions and were told to stay after school.

"That wasn't fair," Doreen said on the playground. "Sister Mary F. doesn't do that. Where is she?"

"In the kitchen, learning obedience," Patricia Walsh said. "Mother Superior is punishing her for taking us to the capitol. It serves her right."

"Who says?" Connor demanded.

"That's none of your business, Connor. You watch how you talk." Nose in the air, Patricia walked away.

"It was probably Patricia's mother who complained," Doreen said. "I'll wait outside for you this afternoon."

"No, you go ahead. They will want you there. I'll be along as soon as I can. Don't tell Ma they're keeping me after school. You can just say I had to finish something."

"Sixty-seven into eight hundred ninety-nine. Carry it out to three zeros, write it out twenty-five times, and put your paper on my desk," Sister Mary M. told Connor. "The same for the rest of you."

I'll go to Bertha's house the long way, Connor decided. I'll sneak past the capitol to see if Da is on the steps. She was testing herself, Connor realized. What did she want? she asked herself uneasily. She didn't want to go back to the tenement on Canal Street, not ever, but when she thought of Da living there by himself with no one to look after him, she felt sad. I'll go by this once, Connor told herself, to see if he's out on the steps watching for me.

It seemed like years since she had walked above the Beaverkill. Three boys, she couldn't recognize them, were trying to drag a piece of tin roofing from the stream. What were they going to do with that? Connor wondered. The boys' trousers were wet to their knees. Connor felt a moment's urge to slide down the bank to splash into the Beaverkill and give the boys a hand.

Down at Martinville a crew of men were planting trees where the shacks had been. It will be a proper park someday, Connor thought. Just like Washington Park.

A suffragist Connor hadn't seen before was at the corner of Swan and State with an armful of pamphlets. She wasn't doing any more business than Bertha had done. Connor glanced over to the capitol. The steps were empty. She reached out to take a pamphlet. "And I'll take another for my mother," she said. The woman smiled as she handed her another copy.

Connor paused before she crossed the street. Maybe Senator Phelan and Da would come out together, the way they sometimes did in the afternoon, for a breath of fine Albany air. A man hurried out the door and down the steps, an assemblyman maybe, Connor thought, sneaking out for a pint of beer. The steps were once again empty. Connor waited, then slowly headed to Arbor Hill.

"We're to be messengers all week," Doreen reported. "The women here and wherever else they are staying in

143

Albany are writing letters to their friends asking them to be here next Monday. Women in Philadelphia and Baltimore and even Chicago. Can you imagine, Connor, coming all that way to help Miss Anthony with the vote?"

"What are we supposed to do?" asked Connor. She was cross and hungry—and hurt too, she had to admit, that Da had not been outside. What would she have done, she wondered, if he had appeared? Skipped out of sight or gone on to talk to him? If he hadn't said he was sorry, she would have known that he didn't really care and would do the same again when he was drunk. If he really cares, Connor thought, Da will find out where we are and come to say he is sorry and please come home. But to a regular house this time where everything would be better.

Doreen was saying something about gathering up the letters from all over town and taking them to the post office. "All right," Connor said. "As soon as I have some milk. Where's Ma?"

"She and Bessie are in the laundry room. Miss Catherine is in the kitchen."

"There's cake in the cupboard," Catherine said. "Help yourself. When you come back from the street you and Doreen can do the supper with me. I'll take care of the tea. Doreen says she can go home late this week."

"We won't be taking tea with Miss Anthony?" Connor asked.

Catherine shook her head impatiently. "We all have our work cut out for us this week, Connor. On Saturday we can let up. On your way now. Bertha gave Doreen a list of where our women are staying. Be sure to get all the letters to the post office by six."

By Friday night Connor was exhausted. For hours after
school she and Doreen tramped the streets of Albany, then
rushed back to Ten Broeck Street to help with supper, or
dinner, as Miss Catherine called it, afterward. She took a
lamp to the room and tried to do homework before she
dropped off to sleep.

Friday night was different. After supper when Doreen
had left and the women had gone to their rooms, Bertha
said Aunt Susan wanted to see Ma and Connor in the
library. Catherine and Bertha would be there, too. There
was something they had to discuss together.

Aunt Susan was very tired, Connor saw at once. Her eyes
slowly closed behind her spectacles, then snapped open,
only to close again. "I'll have a cup of coffee, Mrs. O'Shea,
if you would be so kind. Thank the Lord Monday is at
hand, and I can be on my way. No offense, Bertha, but I
could never abide sitting in one place for very long."

Aunt Susan took a sip of the coffee. "Bertha and I had an
idea—it was really Bertha's idea, which she shared with me. I
suppose she figured she needed my advice, which is silly, of
course, because Bertha has a fine head on her shoulders."

"Aunt Susan," Bertha broke in.

"All right, Bertha, I'll get on with it. Mrs. O'Shea, has
your husband attempted to get in touch with you?"

Connor's mother shook her head.

"Do you think he will?"

"I don't know, ma'am. Perhaps, when the excitement
is past."

"Have you seen your father, Connor?" Miss Anthony
asked next.

145

"No," Connor replied.

Aunt Susan kept looking at her. There was that little smile on her face.

"I went by the capitol Tuesday after school, like I used to. But I didn't see him."

"What did you intend to do, Connor?"

"I don't know," Connor said, confused. "I thought maybe he was lonely to see me, and I guess I was lonely to see him. But I didn't want to go back to Canal Street with him. I just wished it could have been different."

Susan B. Anthony nodded her little nod to let Connor know she understood. "Well," she said, "in spite of Bertha's optimism and our hard labors here in Albany, the delegates, I fear, are not going to decide in our favor."

"You can't be sure, Aunt Susan," Bertha said.

"No, I can't. Why don't you continue, Bertha?"

"I was thinking," Bertha began. "I have this enormous house, which is much too large for Catherine and me, and I thought if the motion doesn't pass, New York will still be the most important state in the union for the suffrage movement and we must keep working at it here until it does pass. Anyway, I told Aunt Susan we could then use the house as a center for the suffrage movement. Aunt Susan agrees. So does Catherine.

"And I thought we could ask Nora to be our housekeeper and live with us, unless she has something else to do. And if she decides to join Mr. O'Shea, there's plenty for a man to do here as well."

"What do you say, Mrs. O'Shea?" Aunt Susan interrupted. "You would be protected here from any trouble Mr. O'Shea might choose to make."

146

"I don't know, miss. It's a fine idea, I think, and I am agreeable. I guess it depends on Connor. What do you say, child?"

Before Connor could reply, Bertha spoke up. "Catherine and I thought you might like to attend Miss Pugh's academy when you finish at Saint Stephen's. And afterward you might think about going to college."

"It's educated women this country needs," Susan B. Anthony said. "Of all the suffragists here in the city, I'd calculate not more than half a dozen have a college education."

"And Da?" Connor asked. "Could I go by the capitol sometimes to talk to him if he wanted to see me? Would that be all right, Ma?"

"That is for you to decide, Connor. Your da is not a bad man, but he is not a good man when he is at the drink."

"Then I'd like to stay here. It will be an adventure, won't it, Ma? An adventure for the two of us, just like you said?"

CHAPTER THIRTY-TWO

By dawn the crazy women had begun to arrive at the capitol building, some alighting from streetcars, others from carriages, while other women marched along the sidewalks from the many sides of Albany. Some were silent, others talked softly, and all were serious as they filled the capitol square.

The women were dressed in black, a bit of white lace at the collar, perhaps, or a red rose on the shoulder. Every woman wore a bonnet with a red ribbon.

Bertha Hall moved among the gathering women. "Along both sides of every sidewalk leading to the state house," she called, "every single sidewalk. Do not obstruct the passage. Let the fine gentlemen pass easily to do their duty. And, please, Aunt Susan urges, not a word, not a sound. But never take your gaze from them as they approach and pass you by."

"You may be tardy today to school," Ma told Connor.

148

"Put on your dark Sunday dress. On your head, this." Connor's mother took from the wardrobe a black straw red-ribboned bonnet. "It's Miss Bertha's. She said you might wear it if you were of a mind. We'll be sisters, lass." Ma took another hat from the wardrobe, a beautiful dark blue high-crowned bonnet with a wide red ribbon.

"Bertha's?" Connor asked.

"No, indeed. Nora's. From Rubin's with our wash money." Ma laughed. "Now, down to breakfast. We must be there early. Miss Catherine and Bessie and Miss Anthony will be coming along with us."

The lines of women had formed along the sidewalks as far as the eye could see. Bertha darted from side to side, answering questions, giving directions and assurances. "Here, Aunt Susan," she indicated. "At the end of the line closest to the capitol steps. You there, Connor, next to her."

As the bells of St. Stephen's rang eight, the squad of capitol policemen marched smartly down State Street, followed closely by Senator Phelan and a group of well-dressed men. Da caught sight of Connor and Ma. He seemed to miss half a step, and his face twitched into a frown or a smile, Connor couldn't tell which, before he pushed out his chest and strode on, heels pounding on the pavement.

The sun rose above the lingering morning mist. Connor breathed the fine Albany air. It smelled, as always in the spring, of moist earth, the river, horses, and the tanneries. From across the square Doreen waved. She was with her father and mother. She pointed to herself, then to Connor and the others. "She wants to come with us," Connor translated.

149

Aunt Susan gave her little nod and Connor waved yes. Doreen ran to join them. "Did you see my father?" she exclaimed. "He said he'd better be here so you wouldn't think suffrage was altogether a woman's business. He's not for the vote yet, he says, but soon. He said Senator Phelan didn't play fair and that wasn't right. Anyway, he's not the only man. Look over there."

Here and there in the long lines, men stood upright in their dark suits and bowler hats, a few with red roses in their lapels.

Toward nine the delegates began to arrive. They looked surprised, and hurried between the lines of women. Some men stared defiantly at the women; others, head down, avoided the women's gazes. As the men passed Aunt Susan, she gave each one a sharp glance, an ironic smile playing at her lips.

Connor looked along the lines. She saw a familiar figure. "Sister," she cried. "It's Sister Mary Francis. Look, Aunt Susan, that's our teacher. In the nun's habit."

"So that's the famous Sister Mary Francis, is it? Well, that means the Lord is on our side." Aunt Susan laughed. "We'll need His help today."

When the last delegate arrived, Da closed the doors to the capitol. He and his men stood in front. The sun rose higher. "It's hot, Ma," Connor whispered. Her mother nodded. She put her hand on Connor's shoulder. "Stand firm, child."

The bells tolled ten. A heavy knock echoed from the doors. The policemen gathered four on each side of the doorway. Connor's father opened the doors wide. A small red-haired man marched to the edge of the steps. "The motion to amend," Senator Phelan shouted, "has failed."

The delegates streamed from the building, hastened down the steps, and scurried toward the sidewalk. "Shame, sir," Susan B. Anthony said clearly to the first man to pass. Along the lines the cries of "Shame!" followed the delegates as they fled the capitol. Senator Phelan disappeared into the shadows of the capitol. Connor's father paused to gaze around the square before he followed the senator inside, drawing the heavy doors closed behind him.

Susan B. Anthony picked up her suitcase. She shook hands with Catherine, Bessie, and Nora. "Thank you," she said simply. "I'm off to California." She looked down at Connor and Doreen. "You know where that is, don't you? It's on the way to Washington."

"I'll take your bag," Connor said.

"The day I can't carry my own suitcase is the day I give up on suffrage for women," Aunt Susan said. "But you and Doreen can come along to the station to keep me company."

The crowd of women parted to let the old woman and the children through. Bertha lifted her hand and motioned the women to fall in behind. "Mine eyes have seen the glory," Bertha's strong voice sang.

The voices of the crazy women swelled, "of the coming of the Lord./He is trampling out the vintage where the grapes of wrath are stored./He hath loosed the fateful lightning of His terrible swift sword./His truth is marching on./Glory, glory hallelujah,/glory, glory hallelujah,/glory, glory hallelujah,/His truth is marching on."

At the front of the marching women Aunt Susan shifted

151

her suitcase from one hand to the other. "It *is* a tad heavy this morning," she said to Connor. "You carry it halfway to the station, and Doreen will carry it the rest of the way. We'll be certain to get to Washington with your help." Susan B. Anthony put her arms around the two girls and set her face steady toward the station.